THE THREE
"We Inves_____

*

Jupiter Jones, Founder

*

Pete Crenshaw, Associate

*

Bob Andrews, Associate

The Three Investigators
Crimebusters
available in Armada

1 Hot Wheels
2 Murder to Go
3 Rough Stuff
4 Funny Business
5 An Ear for Danger
6 Hollywood Horror
7 Reel Trouble
8 Shoot the Works
9 Foul Play
10 Long Shot

THE THREE INVESTIGATORS ™

9
Foul Play

Peter Lerangis
based on characters created by Robert Arthur

Armada
An Imprint of HarperCollins*Publishers*

First published in the U.S.A in 1990
by Random House, Inc.
First published in Great Britain in 1990 in Armada

Armada is an imprint of HarperCollins Children's Division,
part of HarperCollins Publishers Ltd,
77-85 Fulham Palace Road, Hammersmith, London W6 8JB

Printed and bound in Great Britain
by HarperCollins Manufacturing Ltd, Glasgow

1

Return of a Rogue

"DON'T DO IT, JUPE!" PETE CRENSHAW WARNED. HIS dark eyes stared intently across the table at Jupiter Jones.

Pete's girlfriend, Kelly Madigan, clutched his arm, shaking her head sadly. "You're too young to die, Jupe."

"Is there a doctor in the house?" Bob Andrews asked.

He cast a glance around the packed interior of the trendiest food-stop in the Rocky Beach Shopping Mall. His tanned face reflected the light of the neon BUD'S HEALTHWORKS sign, which curved around a bank of video monitors showing old reruns. The blaring laugh tracks seemed to mock his concern.

Jupiter raised an eyebrow. He tried not to glare at Pete or Bob. It was one of the last days of their summer vacation, and he wanted to savor every minute of it. Besides, he *was* the founder of The Three Investigators—the most successful trio of detectives in Rocky

Beach, California—and there was a certain dignity he had to maintain. Even when the guys were once again mocking his food.

He stuffed the loose alfalfa sprouts into the side of his cold soy burger. This was the specialty of the house. But only dedicated dieters like Jupe ever ordered it. "I am going to eat this," Jupe said firmly, waving the burger for emphasis. An orange glob of ginger and burdock root sauce oozed out from the wrinkled grayish mass in the bun. It dripped down his arm, but Jupiter pretended not to notice. "And I am going to enjoy it, no matter how much you taunt me."

With an expression that was equal parts pain and righteousness, the hefty guy lifted the burger to his mouth. His eyes betrayed not even a flicker of agony as he took a bite.

"He did it!" Bob whispered incredulously.

Pete heaved his athletic shoulders and sighed. "Some diet, Jupe," he said, pushing aside his bacon cheeseburger. "You eat, I lose weight. Just watching you kills my appetite."

"Ummm unnnhhhg," Jupe mumbled. He quickly swallowed, cleared his throat, and tried again: "Come on. You three are being so . . . so American. A macrobiotic diet is the perfect combination of yin and yang, the most natural balance of food energies. This stuff has nourished Eastern societies for centuries."

"I thought so," Bob said. "It *looks* like it's been sitting around that long."

A roar of laughter prevented Jupiter from answering. He turned to see a group of about ten people at a round table, howling at the TV show on the monitor above them.

He glanced at the monitor and muttered, "Oh, please, no . . ."

"What gives?" Kelly asked.

Jupiter listlessly speared a warm oat-bran croquette with his fork. "Look what they're watching."

"Hey, it's *The Wee Rogues*, the show that put Jupiter Jones on the map!" Bob said, grinning.

At the sound of the TV show's name, Jupiter cringed. It was so many years ago—fourteen, to be exact—that Jupe had been a child star on *The Wee Rogues*. Back then it had seemed like a piece of cake. All he had to do was be himself, a precocious three-year-old with the vocabulary of a college grad. Somehow, without even trying, he had been able to make people laugh uproariously.

Now, as a teenager, Jupe knew why. One glimpse of the overweight, overconfident toddler said it all: people were laughing *at* him. In show-biz language, he was a sight gag.

Out of the corner of his eye Jupe saw the image of a ten-year-old bully entering the scene behind young Jupe. With a mischievous grin the older boy carefully poured glue over a seat that Jupe was about to sit on.

"Whoa! Get a load of that!" someone at the round table shouted, pointing at the screen.

"That does it," Jupe announced, pushing aside his meal. "I think it's time to move on!"

"Wait a second. That's Buzz Newman," Bob said, nodding toward the other table. "He's a drummer in one of Sax's bands. Great guy, too!" He stood up. "Come on, I'll introduce you!"

"But—but—" Jupe sputtered as Pete and Kelly got up and followed Bob to the table. Bob always seemed to run into rock musicians he knew. His blond good looks and neat, preppy exterior masked the rock 'n' roll fanatic he really was. In Bob's part-time job with Sax Sendler's Rock-Plus talent agency he met all the hottest local players.

But why couldn't Bob just ignore this guy right now? Jupiter wondered.

Jupiter forced himself to stand up and hold his head high. No one at the table could possibly recognize him. . . .

"You were a ham even then!" a guy with long red hair called out at the table.

Jupiter blanched. But the guy was looking at someone else. Across the table a young man with handsome, chiseled features smiled sheepishly.

"Hey, what's the buzz, Buzz?" Bob called out to the red-haired taunter.

Buzz turned around and smiled. "Hi, Bob! Take a seat. We're just checking out our friend George's TV debut!"

"Hey, come on!" Buzz's friend pleaded. "These guys don't even know me."

Kelly looked closely at him. "Hey, I saw you interviewed on TV last night! You're the star of that new musical at the Garber Theater!"

He nodded, his blue eyes lighting up. "*Danger Zone*. Yeah, that's me . . ."

Another burst of laughter went up from the table. "Unfortunately," he continued, looking forlornly at the TV monitor, "that's me up there, too. I'm never going to live this down."

Jupiter scrutinized the screen. He blocked out the painful memory of walking around helplessly glued to a chair. Instead he focused on the face of the bully. The name of the young actor was coming back to him. . . .

"Georgie Brandon!" Jupiter exclaimed.

"*Georgie?*" Buzz echoed.

"That's what they called him back then."

George gave Jupiter a wary look. "How did you know that?"

"I . . . uh . . ." Jupiter noticed that everyone at the table was staring at him. He cleared his throat. "I played the youngest kid in that show."

"You mean *you* were Baby Fatso?" asked a blond girl at the other end of the table.

The mention of that name—especially by a pretty girl—sent a chill up Jupiter's spine. "To be precise, I was *not* Baby Fatso. I played a character by that name."

"I remember you!" George exclaimed. He stood and extended his hand. "You were the smartest little kid I ever saw. Friendly, too."

Jupiter smiled modestly as he shook George's hand. "Well . . . I was just being myself."

"You know, that was my only appearance on *The Wee Rogues*, but it changed my whole life. I got an agent and began hitting it big in commercials. Then they discovered I had a great voice, and . . . well . . ." He smiled and shrugged. "The rest is history."

For a moment Jupiter wanted to remark that George's ego seemed to have grown with age. But he decided to be more polite. "I'm a bit out of touch with show business these days. What are you up to?"

"Out of touch? You must have been out of the galaxy, pal!" George laughed. "Just kidding. The papers have been full of articles about us. *Danger Zone's* the biggest, most expensive musical ever produced in L.A.—laser lights, incredible martial arts displays, and a hot love story, starring guess who!"

Buzz nodded. "I'm drumming in the show's orchestra. You wouldn't believe how much money the producers keep pouring into this show—redesigning costumes, reconstructing the stage, changing the dance numbers, hiring new people. We've been doing the show for over a month, and they keep postponing the opening date."

"Wait a minute," Pete said. "If you're already doing

the show, you must have opened, right? So what's this about an opening date?"

"Oh, we're still in previews," Buzz said. "Before a show opens, there are usually a few weeks of preview performances. They give everyone a chance to see how the show plays to an audience and where the problems are. Sometimes new scenes appear overnight. When all the kinks are worked out, it's time for opening night. That's when the reviewers are invited."

"*If* that day ever comes," George added.

"Your show's in bad shape, huh?" Bob said.

George shook his head. "No, they just think they can make it *perfect*. They're dying to move the show to Broadway someday. And if the show is a hit in New York, that means national tours, film contracts—you know, big bucks."

A handsome dark-haired guy spoke up from across the table. "That's not the *only* reason the previews were extended, George!"

George flashed a guilty grin. "Thanks, Vic. Let's not get into that, okay? I'm trying to make a good impression here."

"Anybody want dessert or coffee?" a waitress's voice piped up.

The Three Investigators and Kelly pulled up seats around the table. As the others gave their orders, George turned to Jupiter. "What have *you* been up to all these years, buddy?"

Jupiter reached into his pocket, pulled out a card, and gave it to George.

A change of expression passed across George's face. It was nothing an average person would detect— just a slight drop of his smile, a flicker of concern. But it didn't escape the trained eye of Jupiter Jones.

"We should talk sometime," Jupiter said.

"Yeah," George replied, his eyes darting left and right. "Like now."

George rose from the table and dug a few five-dollar bills out of his jeans pocket. Placing them on the table, he said to Buzz, "This'll cover me. I'm going to go shoot the breeze with my old pal for a while."

Buzz nodded absently and returned to a deep conversation he'd started with Bob. Two or three of the girls were leaning across the table, listening intently to the blond Investigator. Jupiter never ceased to be amazed at his friend's ability to attract the opposite sex without even trying.

A chorus of good-byes arose from the table as George began to leave.

Jupiter signaled Pete with his eyes. He tried to catch Bob's eye, too, but failed. Bob would have to be filled in later. Kelly was so busy talking to another girl that she never noticed Pete leave.

Jupiter and Pete followed George to the end of a corridor in the mall. They stopped beyond a pile of sawdust and wooden planks near a shop that hadn't yet opened. George looked around.

"Okay, there's nobody here," he said. "I don't want to take any chances." He looked straight at Jupiter. "You're really detectives? This is no joke?"

"I give you my word," Jupiter replied.

George lowered his voice. "I hope I can trust you. As you've probably already guessed, I'm in trouble. Big trouble."

Jupiter found George's melodramatic tone amusing. He nodded knowingly. "Someone's after your job, huh?"

George shook his head. "Someone's after my life."

"Why?" Pete asked in disbelief.

"If I knew, I wouldn't have brought you here!" George snapped. "The last week or so I've been getting these bizarre letters and calls—"

"What kind of calls?" Jupiter interrupted.

George shrugged. "Sometimes just a hang-up.

Sometimes a gravelly voice that says 'You're gonna get it!' Other times it's a British accent, kind of an old-person's voice that says 'Beware, thespian!' *Thespian* is an old-fashioned word for actor."

"Yes, I know," Jupiter said. "Go on."

"The worst type is a loud cackle that could be a man's or a woman's voice—I can't tell."

"What about the letters?" Jupiter asked. "What do they say?"

"Real psycho stuff, man," George replied, shuddering. "Weird messages about how I'm going to die in a throne of blood, something about a forest moving in to swallow me up . . ."

"Maybe if we look at the letters," Jupe said, "we can spot some clues to the sender's identity."

Suddenly George looked crestfallen. "Oh, boy. Guess what genius threw them out."

"Whoops," Pete said.

George shrugged. "I don't know, they were just so . . . *creepy*. I figured they were harmless, from some demented fan—but that was before the accidents started happening."

"Accidents?" Jupiter asked.

"Scenery falling, nails and razor blades mysteriously appearing on the stage floor where I'm supposed to do a dance number." George's eyes were ablaze with fear and determination. "Look, I need help. I've wanted to get hold of a private eye, but I held off. It would be too obvious to have a strange older dude hanging around backstage. But three young guys—I could say you're my friends. It would be perfect! Tell me you'll take the case. I *need* you guys."

Pete glanced at Jupiter. Immediately Pete saw a familiar look in his friend's eyes, a barely contained excitement that a new case was brewing.

"We'll do it on one condition," Jupiter told George.

"Name it."

"You've got to keep our identities a secret," Jupiter insisted. "In case this is an inside job."

A grateful grin stretched across George's face. "It's a deal! Meet me in my dressing room tonight around six. I don't have to be in makeup till seven thirty, so that'll give me some time to show you around. In fact, if you get there by five thirty, you can see me do a TV interview in front of the theater." He clasped Jupiter's hand, then Pete's. "This is fantastic. I can't believe I ran into you!"

Shaking George's hand, looking into his fiery eyes, Jupiter began to feel a clutch of excitement in his gut. He hadn't felt that way since childhood, since the year he spent on a sound stage.

He had grown to hate show business since then. The Baby Fatso thing was just too embarrassing. But now he realized something he'd never before admitted.

Show business was in his blood. And he couldn't wait to sink his teeth into this case.

2

Danger Sign

JUPITER DROVE OVER TO PETE'S HOUSE LATE THAT afternoon to pick him up for the theater.

Kelly opened Pete's front door before Jupiter had a chance to ring the bell. "Hi, Jupe," she said, adjusting the shoulder straps of her dress.

Jupiter smiled uncertainly. "I didn't think *you'd* want to come. You realize we're on a *case*—"

"No problem," Kelly replied. "I just want to be the first of my friends to see *Danger Zone!*"

"Right. Where's Pete?"

"Upstairs. He had this idea he could go to the theater in jeans and a T-shirt. He got a little nervous when he saw what I was wearing. And then when he saw *you* walking toward the house, he ran up to change."

Closing the door behind him, Jupiter stepped into the living room. "Well, I suppose jeans are fine, but I prefer a little formality." As he spoke, his black bow tie bobbed with the movement of his Adam's apple.

"You look cute in a suit," Kelly said.

Jupe squirmed. He was relieved to hear Pete bounding down the stairs. The cuffs of Pete's shirt peeked out from the sleeves of his blue blazer, which fit a little too snugly around his muscular chest.

"Last time I wore this was when I accepted my junior varsity letter," Pete said. He began to stretch, but stopped when he heard a small ripping sound. "Oops. Guess I've grown. Come on, let's go pick up the car. The shop closes in fifteen minutes."

"The shop?" Jupiter barely had time to register his surprise as Pete and Kelly sped out the door. "Wait a minute! Why can't we use my wheels? They're right here!"

Pete glanced briefly at the rundown pickup truck Jupiter had borrowed from his Uncle Titus and Aunt Mathilda's junkyard. "Uh, no offense, Jupe, but we're part of the audience, not the sideshow."

Jupiter trotted across the lawn and caught up with Pete and Kelly at the sidewalk. "At least it's working."

"So's mine," Pete said. "It's a great one, Jupe—a vintage Toyota Corolla with only sixty thousand miles. I picked it up at the police auction yesterday. This morning I dropped it off for inspection."

"Inspection?" Jupiter stopped in his tracks. "What if it doesn't pass? It's almost five o'clock and we—"

Pete laughed. "Don't sweat it. The car drives fine, the lights work. All the shop might need to do is fix up some minor stuff." He winked. "Besides, I know the mechanic."

"I've heard this before," Kelly said. She grabbed

both of their arms. "Come on, guys, we better move it."

Jupe sped them in the pickup to the Rocky Beach Auto Diagnostic Center. Pete opened the glass door of the garage, shouting, "Hey, Al! How's my new dream machine?"

A forest of steel hydraulic lifts greeted them. On top of each rested an automobile, casting a shadow on the floor. From the farthest corner a sleepy-eyed mechanic rose from an old vinyl armchair. He nodded to Pete, then took a quick look at the clock on the wall.

"Hooo-doggy! Is it five o'clock already? I must have nodded off. How can I help you, son?"

"I came to pick up my car," Pete said. "It's the steel-gray Toyota, remember?"

Al scratched his head and looked up at the cars. "Steel-gray Toyota . . . steel-gray Toyota . . ." He pointed. "You mean that one?"

Their shoulders sank. At the top of one of the lifts was Pete's car, with work lights and wrenches hanging from the bottom. Greasy rags were strewn around on the floor below.

"Wh-what did you do to it?" Pete asked in dismay.

Al shrugged. "I didn't do nothing to it. You got a worn-out Pitman arm. Can't pass inspection with that."

"A worn-out *what*?"

"It's like this." He pointed to the long rod that connected the two tires. "That's the steering linkage, which turns the wheels. But something has to turn *it* back and forth—and that's the Pitman arm. It connects the linkage to the steering gearbox, which is connected to the steering column, which connects to the steering wheel." He gave a gap-toothed smile. "The Pitman arm's made of metal, but it doesn't last forever, you know."

"Well, go ahead and put another one on," Pete said.

Al shook his head. "Can't. Don't keep 'em in stock. Nobody does. Gotta order it from the manufacturer—could take two, maybe three weeks." He chuckled and began to walk away. "Hope you got another means of transport, 'cause this baby can't leave the shop now."

"Just for the night, Al, as a favor?" Pete pleaded.

"No way, José," Al countered. "You can't drive around without an inspection sticker—unless you like paying tickets. Anyway, I threw out the old Pitman arm."

"*What?* How could you—"

"The car, my friend, is staying here. Catch my drift?"

Pete looked at the ground. "Right . . . uh, thanks, Al."

As he skulked back to the pickup, he kept his eyes averted from Kelly's accusing glare.

◆　　◆　　◆

"Yeeow! Easy, Jupe! Didn't anyone ever teach you to drive *around* potholes?" Pete rubbed his head in pain and sank lower in the front seat of the pickup truck.

"Sorry, Pete, I didn't see it," Jupiter replied.

Squeezed between the two of them, Kelly shifted uncomfortably. "You know, I'm *glad* Bob couldn't make it. If there were four of us in here, we'd all be basket cases by now."

"He's the one having a good time," Pete muttered. "Sitting in a club, checking out some new band for Sax—what a job."

"Have patience, Pete," Jupiter said. "We're almost there."

Jupiter steered around the next corner. In the distance two large white vans were parked at the curb by a large theater. A network of wires snaked along the street between them, held in place by thick, silver-colored tape. Cameramen swarmed around the area, shouting instructions and adjusting lights. Above the entire scene a crane lowered an enormous rectangular DANGER ZONE sign toward its eventual place on the marquee. Jupiter craned his head out the window to get a better look.

"I guess we made it in time," Pete said. "Looks like they haven't started shooting the TV interview."

"Hey, Jupe!" came George Brandon's voice. Jupe, Pete, and Kelly looked under the marquee. Sitting on a high canvas chair, George waved to them. A man in a black turtleneck fussed with George's hair while a woman dabbed powder onto his forehead. They both looked annoyed as George stood up and called, "Come join the chaos! The camera's about to roll!"

"Places for take one!" a ponytailed, bearded man called out over a bullhorn. "Clear the area, please!"

Jupiter parked the pickup a half-block away. He ran with Pete and Kelly to the front of the theater. There they joined the crowd watching the shoot from behind a line of wooden police barricades.

George waited in position to the right of the marquee. The hairdresser was now spraying the hair of a woman dressed in a ruffled silk shirt and a flowing skirt. As he scurried away, the woman moved toward George, holding a microphone to her mouth. She revealed a dazzling smile to the nearest camera.

"Wow! That's Jewel Coleman from *Showbiz Today!*" Kelly said. "I *love* that show."

"Gossip journalism," Jupiter remarked, rolling his eyes. "Airheads talking about other airheads."

"But the hunky guys she has on . . ." Kelly looked at Jupiter's disdainful expression and Pete's disapproving scowl. "Oh, *you* two wouldn't understand."

The crowd fell silent at the sound of Jewel Coleman's voice. "*Danger Zone*—as most theatergoers know—is the title of a long-awaited musical previewing here at the Garber Theater. It's fun, it's lavish, it's the talk of the trade. But the atmosphere at the Garber is tense these days, and it's not only preopening jitters. Channel One's investigative team has discovered that there have been some strange goings-on, all centered around young heartthrob George Brandon. George, explain something to us—has *Danger Zone* become a *real* danger zone?"

She held the microphone out to George. But as he opened his mouth to speak, his voice was drowned out by a frantic shout from a worker standing near the crane.

"*Yo! Heads up!*"

Jewel Coleman let out a piercing shriek and dove under the marquee. Around her, people scattered into the street, dropping clipboards, sandwiches, and electronic equipment.

Jupiter looked up. The huge DANGER ZONE sign dangled from the crane by only one thin cable. Another cable swung limply in the air, frayed at the place where it too had been holding the sign.

"*George!*" Jupiter blurted out as the sign snapped loose and hurtled toward George Brandon's head!

3

Backstage Bother

"*E*EAAAGH!" GEORGE YELLED. HE THREW HIMSELF TO the sidewalk and rolled into the street.

With a deafening crash the sign shattered on the pavement. Jupiter, Pete, and Kelly covered their faces and ducked.

In the eerie moment of dead silence afterward, Jupiter looked up. The sign was now a heap of jagged plastic shards against the theater wall, about fifteen feet from where George had been standing.

"Is anybody hurt?" Jupe said as soon as he could find his voice.

"No," Pete and Kelly said at the same time.

"What a break," said Pete, surveying the pile of damage. "It landed in the one place where nobody was standing."

"Right," Jupiter said as he began walking toward George. "Although I'm not sure '*break*' is the word I'd have chosen."

The wail of police sirens cut through the evening

air. Left and right the onlookers were brushing themselves off and ogling the broken sign.

Jupiter pushed his way through the crowd surrounding George. Pete and Kelly were close behind him. The cameramen hovered around the group, frantically angling for shots of George's reactions.

"Did you get it all?" a severe-looking silver-haired man asked.

"You bet, C.G.," came a reply from behind one of the cameras. "The works—Brandon's reaction, the impact on the background—"

"Beautiful," C.G. said. "We came for a soft feature and ended up with hard news. Beautiful."

"Excuse me, excuse me," Jupiter called out, elbowing his way forward. He could hear fragments of George's voice but couldn't see him.

"Came from nowhere . . . No, no, I'm fine . . ."

At last Jupiter got to the center of the crowd. But Jewel Coleman had beat him to it. Sitting beside George on the curb, she looked up toward one of the cameras. "Are you on me?"

"Go," the cameraman replied.

Immediately her brow became creased with concern. "As you have seen, captured on camera tonight, *Danger Zone* is living up to its title. George Brandon, how did you feel when you saw that massive sign coming ever closer, inches away from crushing your skull?"

"Crushing?" The color drained from George's face. "Well, it wasn't really that close."

Jewel nodded solemnly. "I'll bet there are quite a few young people relieved that their idol isn't lying mangled beneath that grotesque pile." She gestured toward the sign. "Can we get a closeup of that, Jerry?"

George looked at the sign and swallowed hard. Catching a glimpse of Jupiter, he quickly turned to Jewel and said, "Thank you, but I've got to get to my dressing room." He managed a weak smile. "The show must go on."

With that, he stood up, grabbed Jupiter's arm, and mumbled, "Come with me. Pretend you're a bodyguard or something."

Pete sneaked in front of them. "Okay, clear the deck!" he barked, using the voice he usually reserved for the football field. At the sight of his tall, imposing physique, people quickly cleared a path to the stage door around on the side of the theater.

Jupiter glanced over his shoulder to see Kelly following. The cameramen had retreated down the street, where two police cars had pulled up to the curb.

A burly man with beard stubble was at the stage door, holding it open. "You all right, my man?" he asked George.

"Yeah, Luther, fine," George answered.

Luther eyed Jupiter and Pete suspiciously. "Who are these guys?"

"It's okay, they're friends." George turned to Jupiter with a half-smile. "You are looking at the world's greatest doorman. This guy wouldn't let in the President without prior clearance."

Luther's grim face broke into a shy, gap-toothed smile. "Come on, get inside before I lock *you* out," he said.

The four of them slipped inside the theater, leaving the chaotic sounds outside. "Follow me," George said, leading the others down a short corridor. A large corkboard hung on the wall, every inch covered by notices held in place with thumbtacks. Next to it, the wall was defaced by a jumble of hastily scribbled phone numbers surrounding a telephone.

At the end of the corridor was a half-opened door with the name LUTHER SHARPE on it. Jupiter could see keys hanging from a pegboard on the inside of the door. To the right of Luther's office another door led to the stage.

"Hold on," Luther called out as George ushered the others down the corridor. "You got some company in your dressing room, and I don't think they want any strangers in there."

George turned back. "Who?"

"Mr. Firestone and Mr. Crocker."

"Well, well, the producer *and* the main investor, in my humble room," George said. "What did I do to have this honor? Did they say anything to you, Luther?"

Luther shrugged. "A little. They rushed out when they heard the noise, and when they saw you were okay, they just told me, 'Make sure he gets in here in one piece.' "

"That's what I like about them—their incredible sensitivity," George remarked. He turned toward the door to the stage. "All right, looks like I'll have to meet the intruders head-on. Once more into the breach!" He held up his right arm as if he were brandishing a sword, then ran through the doorway.

Pete gave Jupiter a puzzled look.

"That's a line from Shakespeare," Jupiter explained. "Spoken by King Henry the Fifth to his men as they go into battle."

"Great," Pete said flatly.

"Which reminds me," Jupe went on. "Remember George said he got letters threatening he'd die on a throne of blood and that a forest would come swallow him up?"

"Yeah," Pete said, "weird stuff."

"Well, that rings a faint bell. I think it's from a play."

"So?" Pete said.

"So that's our first real clue."

"You mean—the sender is from the theater world?" asked Kelly.

"Most likely," Jupe said, and led the way through the door into the backstage area.

"Just wait outside the closed door to your right," Luther called after them. "And keep off the stage."

Jupiter turned right and walked backstage. The area

was dark and cluttered with baskets of clothes, tables covered with tools, and one side of a fake car. To his left, the stage shone under the bright glare of spotlights.

To his right, a shiny metallic star hung on a wooden door in a nearby corner. Underneath it was a plastic nameplate that read GEORGE BRANDON. Jupiter, Pete, and Kelly walked closer to it, until the sound of angry voices inside made them stop.

"Oops," Pete said. "Those guys don't sound happy."

"I'm going to do a little exploring," Jupiter said. "You two keep your ears open." He nodded at George's closed door. "Call me when those guys leave."

"Right," Pete replied.

Jupe wandered into one of the wings, an area to the side of the stage. He watched silently as carpenters, technicians, and stagehands ran about. The sound of electric drills competed with voices shouting into walkie-talkies.

Jupiter could feel his heart quicken. There was something about the noise, the warmth of the lights, the vastness of the rows of empty seats. Ordinary life seemed miles away. Here, sheltered inside the theater, an army of dedicated professionals was going about the task of creating a fantasy.

To the rear of the stage an enormous backdrop began to rise off the floor. It was a replica of an underground cavern wall, covered with rocks and eerie hidden lights. Rivulets of water flowed among the crags. Jupiter realized at once it was a masterpiece of plaster and papier-mâché. Behind it, stagehands in old work clothes pulled ropes that extended upward into the darkness. They were raising the backdrop into the fly space, where it could hang out of the audience's sight. As the cavern backdrop went up, a different backdrop came down to take its place.

Jupe turned toward the front curtain, and a flickering electronic light caught his attention. Peeking out from behind an inner curtain was a chest-high control board. It was covered with buttons, switches, and a computer keyboard. Above it a monitor rested on a wooden shelf bolted to the wall. A set of headphones hung on a hook near the monitor.

Jupiter looked both ways. Everyone seemed preoccupied. To Jupiter computers were fun—he spent days hacking away on his own computers. So as long as he had to wait, he might as well poke around this one. He stepped quietly to the control board and looked at the screen.

<u>DANGER ZONE</u>
GARBER THEATER, LOS ANGELES
SOUND, LIGHT, AND FLY CUES
J. BERNARDI, SM
J. EVERSON, ASM

| 1 | LIGHT | AK RAISES HAND |
| 2 | SOUND | AK: "LAST PERSON ON EARTH!" |

```
3  SOUND    SIGNAL FROM ORCH. CONDUCTOR
4  LIGHT    BOYS AT CENTER STAGE

         --  Press Return to continue  --
_____
            Use cursor to highlight cue
   F1:  Command menu    F2:  Edit menu
         F3:  Add line    F4:  Reorder
```

Jupiter began fiddling with the keyboard. The screen scrolled up and down, flickered from menu to menu.

"Yo!" came a sudden loud voice.

Jupiter's fingers snapped off the keyboard. He spun around.

Coming toward him was a young stagehand with long blond hair and a thick beard stubble. The sleeves of his faded flannel shirt were rolled up, revealing a tattoo.

"What do you think you're doing, pal?" he demanded, his green eyes glowering suspiciously.

Jupiter studied him closely for a moment. "The guy who warned George," he finally said.

"What?"

"You're the guy who yelled at George just before the sign fell down. I remember your face."

"Yeah, well, you better get your face out of here. You got no business at that computer. You ain't the stage manager."

Jupiter nodded. "A valid observation. I'll return the screen to normal." He turned back to the computer—

and immediately felt a heavy hand grip him by the shoulder and yank him back.

"Hey!" the stagehand yelled. "Did you hear me, buddy? Read my lips: Get lost!"

Glancing at the sooty smudge the guy's hand had left on his shoulder, Jupiter calmly said, "Perhaps you could contain your wrath for a moment while I attempt to explain—"

"Look, I ain't got time to listen to you and your ten-dollar words. If you don't get out of here right now, wimp, I'll haul your fat behind out myself!" He reached for Jupiter again.

Jupiter backed away. He could feel the blood rising from his toes to his head. He was becoming furious. "I'd advise you to keep your hands off me."

The stagehand was grinning. "No . . . wimp ain't the right word. *Blimp* is more like it!" This time he shoved Jupiter.

Jupiter stumbled but stayed on his feet. Enraged, he looked up to see the stagehand approaching with clenched fists. "I warned you," Jupiter said, springing into a defensive judo stance.

A low chuckle escaped from the stagehand. "Would you get a load of this?"

He leaned back into a perfect *kokutsu-dachi* stance, his feet flat and perpendicular, his forward arm raised toward Jupiter.

Before Jupiter could react, the stagehand lunged at him with a quick, straightforward *seiken* punch.

Jupiter skillfully moved out of the way. Scrambling

into position, he stepped into a tangle of ropes in a darkened corner.

"Who-oa!" With a dull thud Jupe landed on the floor.

He looked up—just in time to see the underside of the stagehand's boot flying at him!

4

Dressing Room Drama

"*HEY!*"
Jupiter was barely aware of the other voice, or the footsteps racing toward him. He wasn't even sure how he managed to twist away.

But somehow, when his attacker's boot came crashing to the floor, Jupiter's face wasn't there to greet it.

Huddled several feet away near a pile of coiled rope, Jupiter breathed a brief sigh of relief. His martial arts technique may have failed him, but he was still in one piece.

"Knock it off, Bruno!" The new voice belonged to a tall man with a full head of white hair, wearing a crew-neck sweater and khaki pants. His deep-set eyes were wide with bewilderment. Behind him were Pete and Kelly.

Pete reached down to help Jupiter stand up. "You all right, Jupe?"

"Fine," Jupiter said, brushing himself off, "considering I was almost decapitated by Mr. Cordiality here."

"You better watch yourself, Bruno," the white-haired man said, "if you want to keep your job!"

"Aw, come on, Jim, I wasn't really gonna hit the dude—I just wanted to scare him," Bruno said. "He wouldn't stop messing with your computer. He doesn't belong back here, anyway."

"He happens to be a friend of George's, all right? Now get back to work. I'll handle this."

As the stagehand left, the man extended his hand to Jupiter. "Jim Bernardi," he said with a nasal accent that made his name sound like "Buhnawdi." "I'm the stage manager. I was chatting with your friends here when we heard the noise. Sorry about that."

Stage manijuh . . . chattin' wid ya' frens heeah . . . Jupiter prided himself on his ability to recognize accents, and this one was unmistakable. "Are you from New York City?" he asked.

"Brooklyn, by way of Long Island." *Loo-awn Guylind.* "How did you know?"

"Just guessed. Thanks for saving me."

"Hey, no problem. Listen, if Bruno gives you any more trouble, you just let me know."

"That's all right," Jupiter said with a laugh. "I guess I deserved it for snooping around."

Bernardi smiled. "If snooping around's what you want, snooping around's what you'll get! What do you want to see first?"

"Can you give us a tour?" Kelly asked.

"No prob. Follow me."

Jupiter could see a look of profound disinterest in Pete's eyes. "I think I'll stick around George's dressing room," Pete said. "In case those guys leave." He eagerly grabbed a sports magazine that was lying on a nearby table and sat against the wall.

Jupiter nodded, but his mind was already racing ahead, assembling questions. Who was this Bruno character, and did he know anything about the attempts on George's life? Was that why he was standing by the crane when the sign fell, and why he tried to intimidate Jupiter?

Or was George's persecutor someone else, someone who could easily make things go wrong backstage?

Like the stage manager.

For that matter, it could be anyone involved with the show. It was best to start slow, find out exactly who handled the props and scenery.

Bernardi led Jupe and Kelly onto the stage. "It's a pretty wild show, about these young American martial arts students who get stuck in Japan just as World War II begins. Your friend George plays their leader, who tries to arrange an escape and ends up becoming part of a spy ring. He leads an incredible rush through ancient temples, underground caverns, you name it."

"Awesome!" Kelly said, her eyes shining.

They watched as several stagehands arranged a set— two sofas and a black lacquer table with a telephone on top of it. A man wearing a headset fussed with the phone, while another walked from place to place, looking up into the balcony. Behind them was a backdrop made to look like a living room wall with bookcases.

"That's a pretty simple set," Jupiter said. "What are all those people doing?"

"Nothing is that simple." Bernardi stopped and gestured upstage toward the back. "Even if this was the only set in the show, it would take . . . let's see . . . at least sixteen full-time employees to set it up and run it."

"*Sixteen?*" Kelly shook her head. "For a living room? Maybe they can come help my parents next time we rearrange the furniture."

Bernardi laughed. "The unions are very strict. Each stagehand can do only one job and no other. Bringing in the set pieces like the furniture, placing the props like the lamp and phone, lighting the lamp, making the phone ring, and so on—a different person does each thing. And you gotta have a substitute for each one of them, in case of emergency—union rule. It adds up to sixteen people all together."

Jupiter whistled with amazement. "How do you coordinate them all during the show?"

"Thought you'd never ask! I'll show you the control board—and this time Bruno won't bother you."

A deep voice echoed across the stage: "Turntable moving!"

"Hang on a second!" Bernardi shouted. He led Jupiter and Kelly over a curved groove that traced a large circle in the floor. "Okay!"

Jupiter watched as the circular section they'd been standing on slowly began to turn. It moved the living room set upstage while another set emerged from behind.

Bernardi walked to the control board and sat on a stool in front of the monitor. "I stand here during the show, wearing this headphone-and-mike set. The instructions to the backstage people are entered into the computer. When they pop up on the screen, I signal them to the right people—we call this kind of signal a 'cue.' For the sound and light people, I just speak over the mike—like 'lights thirty-five, go!' For the fly people—the ones who lower the backdrops—I cue with a flashlight. A few seconds before the cue I turn the flashlight on, as a warning. The workers stand ready. The actual cue is when I flick the light off."

"And the computer allows you to add and change the instructions," Jupiter guessed.

"Well, not *me*," Bernardi said. "I got a guy who comes in and does it for me. Actually, stage managers usually just work with a marked-up script. But for a show this complicated, this centralized computer system was set up. Everything can be programmed from my board—by a computer expert."

"Is it that difficult?" Jupiter asked. "You don't have pull-down menus or macros?"

"You're speaking Greek," Bernardi said with a chuckle. "You have to type in these long, complicated instructions in computerese. If *I* ever tried to do it, the show would be a mess—cars coming into the living room, blackouts during the daytime scenes . . . "

Jupe looked puzzled. "But you give the cues manually, and you can read what they are on your screen. So if something on the screen is wrong, can't you ignore it and give the right one?"

"Of course," Bernardi said. "But in previews, this place is a zoo. Just when you're starting to learn the cues, the designers make huge changes. And you're so busy talking, signaling, answering questions, and arguing during the show, you tend to rely on the computer—which isn't so great if a change hasn't been entered!"

"Pssst!"

Jupe turned and saw Pete frantically motioning to them. Jupe and Kelly excused themselves and ran back to George's dressing room.

"It sounds like World War Three in there," Pete told them. "Maybe we ought to go out for a snack and come back later."

But, mesmerized, the three visitors pressed around the dressing room door to listen.

The first voice was loud and slightly hoarse. "How can you say 'Trust me'? We trusted you the day after your first understudy quit, and you went off to Yosemite that weekend."

"We've been through this, Mr. Firestone." That voice was George's. "You yourself said it was good to do something physical once in a while—"

"Yeah, but *rock climbing*? When you know there's no one to take your place in the show? And did you tell anyone? No! You had to go sprain your leg—and just when sales were starting to pick up."

A deeper voice cut in. "It really hurt us to have to close the show those two weeks. Customers got pretty ticked off—we lost a bundle on refunds, and we still haven't recovered from the bad press. I can't afford to lose any more money on this show. If I pull out now, I can at least cut my losses."

"Easy, Sid," came Firestone's voice. "We've come too far to close the show. There are . . . other options."

"Like hiring Matt Grant to replace me?" snapped George. "The only movie star whose age equals his IQ? Is *that* what you came here to tell me? I thought it was only a rumor."

"Well . . ." Crocker said reluctantly. "We'd be guaranteed good box office."

There was a moment of silence. "Look, it's your investment, Mr. Crocker," George finally said. "Your money makes or breaks *Danger Zone*. If you want someone who can pout and mumble, hire Matt. Your sales will pick up for a few weeks, until people realize they have to bring hearing aids to the theater.

If you want someone who was born to play this role, stay with me. Besides, we have a new understudy."

"Great, so now you can go off hang gliding next weekend, right?" Firestone said.

"I know how you feel about me, Mr. Firestone. But I'm dedicated to this show. I may not be a household name yet, but people come to see *quality* in the live theater. This show will make me a star, and everyone'll say *you* discovered me."

Jupiter felt like cheering George on, but he stayed silent.

"Let's talk about this some other time, when we've all cooled off a little, okay?" Firestone said.

Chairs scraped and feet shuffled. Jupiter, Pete, and Kelly quickly backed away from the door.

"One other thing," George added. "If you're *really* worried about money, think about this: I signed a run-of-the-play contract. If you fire me, you'll not only have to pay Matt's Hollywood-style salary, but you'll have to pay my salary, too, as long as the play runs."

"You never told me that, Manny," Crocker said.

Firestone didn't answer.

There was a slight chuckle from George. "Looks like the only way you'll save money is to keep me in the show—or kill me!"

Some more shuffling, a little grumbling, and the door flew open. Pete and Kelly instantly pretended to be looking at the sports magazine. Jupiter shuffled things on the props table as if he knew what he was doing.

But props were the last thing he was thinking about. He had a sick, nagging feeling in his gut.

A feeling that George had just said the wrong thing to the wrong people.

5

Busted Connection

"GEORGE MAY HAVE JUST PUT OUT THE WELCOME MAT for his own murderer," Jupiter said.

"How's that?" Pete asked.

The two Investigators were conferring outside the "hair room" minutes after eavesdropping on George's argument with the producer. Inside, Kelly watched Lovell Madeira, the hairdresser, trim George's hair.

"Look," Jupe began. "George said he thought someone was after his life. He's had threatening phone calls, letters, mysterious accidents on the set. He was almost beheaded in front of our eyes."

"And?" Pete said.

"*And* George practically begged Mr. Firestone and Mr. Crocker to kill him."

"He was just kidding, Jupe," Pete said.

"I know that," Jupe said. "But those two have everything to gain from getting George out of the show and his contract—permanently. So there's two for the suspect list."

"Check," said Pete.

Jupiter stepped into the hair room. The hairdresser was analyzing Kelly as he trimmed George's hair. "A typical Venusian . . . a delicious concern with her appearance, very sensual—in a healthy way. Tending toward Mars, I think—forceful."

Kelly blushed.

"Quit bugging my friends with this crazy astro-babble!" George said.

Lovell Madeira rolled his eyes. "It has nothing to do with *astrology*, per se. Each of us exhibits certain personality traits associated with the planets—"

"You should know," George said with a mischievous smile. "You're always in orbit."

Lovell held up his scissors in a mock threat. "Don't tempt me!" He brushed George's neck off, then removed the white smock from around his neck. "There—the world's quickest trim."

"Come on, guys," George said, hopping out of the chair. "Let's grab something to eat. I've got almost an hour and a half before makeup at seven thirty."

"All right!" Pete said.

"You mean you're not going to channel with us?" Lovell said to George.

"Going to *what*?" George said.

"Don't you remember? I'm having some of the actors over to my place before the show, for half an hour or so. We're going to reach into our channels, contact past lives . . ."

George grimaced. "Thanks, Lovell, but I'd rather contact a cheeseburger myself."

Lovell chuckled softly as the visitors followed George out of the hair room.

They ran down the stairs and into George's dressing room. For the first time, Jupiter got a clear view of it. The walls seemed to be one big advertisement for George Brandon—newspaper clippings, press releases, framed black-and-white portraits, fan letters. George's brash, smiling face was everywhere.

"Whoa, looks like you're a pretty famous guy," Pete said.

George ripped off his T-shirt, which was now covered with strands of cut hair. He reached for another shirt hanging on a clothes rack. "Well, only among people who're into the theater—and only because I use Ruth Leslie, the best publicity agent in the business!"

"Listen, George," Jupiter said, changing the subject, "we couldn't help but overhear some of that conversation with those two guys."

George grabbed a pair of sunglasses and put them on. "Can we talk about it at the Burger Bistro? This place is giving me the creeps."

Footsteps drummed down the stairwell outside George's door. A group of actors walked by carrying bulky leather or canvas bags over their shoulders. They waved as they passed George's dressing room.

One of them stopped and poked his head in. Jupiter remembered meeting him earlier that day before leaving the mall. He had been introduced as George's understudy. His dark eyes danced with a barely contained enthusiasm. "You coming to Lovell's place, George?"

George looked at him sadly. "*Et tu*, Vic Hammil? Lovell hasn't gotten *you* hooked on this stuff, has he?"

Vic laughed. "Of course! It's the best entertainment this side of watching *you* on *The Wee Rogues*! Lovell gets all worked up, and we make believe we hear voices—it's great! You'd love it."

"Not enough to starve myself before the show," George replied.

"Is *that* what you're worried about?" Vic unzipped his shoulder bag, revealing a large white paper sack. "This'll take care of your hunger. It's from Le Corpulence, that new bakery."

He opened the sack and a warm, sweet, steamy aroma burst out. At the sight of fresh-baked sticky buns glistening with cinnamon and sugar, Jupiter's mouth began to water.

"Come on, it'll be dynamite," Vic urged, the glint in his eyes growing stronger. "It'll loosen you up before the show."

"Whaddaya say, guys?" George asked his visitors.

"It's okay with me," Pete said.

"Me too," Kelly agreed.

Jupiter hesitated. Those sticky buns were definitely not on his diet. But if he went with the others, he might pick up clues about the case. Besides, he didn't have to *eat* those buns. He could just . . . *smell* them.

"Sure, I'll go with you," Jupiter said.

"Then on to contact the spirits!" George said with a flourish.

•   •   •

Jupiter pulled into a parking space in front of a small two-story building. He watched as George and Vic walked through the front door, happily reaching into Vic's bag.

"Great," Jupiter mumbled. "They insist on going in George's car, then they eat all the buns themselves!"

Without waiting for a reaction from Pete and Kelly, he jammed on the parking brake and jumped out of the pickup.

Lovell Madeira met them at the front door. Under a deeply knitted brow, his eyes were distant and distracted. "Take off your shoes, please; I just waxed the floors" were his only words of greeting.

Jupiter, Pete, and Kelly obeyed, walking in stockinged feet through a long, narrow hallway. At the end of it they came into a small, windowless room, lit only by a dim lamp with a heavy cloth shade on a table to the right of the entrance. Various strange charts hung on the walls. Most had to do with planets, stars, and symbols Jupiter didn't recognize. Across the room was a lopsided spinet piano, next to a white marble bust of William Shakespeare on a small wooden table.

On an old Oriental carpet in the center, the group of actors sat in a circle holding hands. Lovell took his place in the circle near the door. He beckoned Jupiter, Pete, and Kelly to sit next to him.

As soon as they did, Lovell began to speak in soft,

measured tones. "Now, close your eyes and let your-selves be a vessel to the forces around you."

Jupiter had no idea what that last part meant, so he just closed his eyes.

"The voices visited me today," Lovell continued. "They said a door will open for one of you tonight. But it's a door that has been hidden away for centuries. I asked who, but they wouldn't say. I asked what kind of former life the door led to, and they fell silent."

One of the actors snickered. The sound hung in the air, strangely out of place.

When Lovell spoke again, it was a deep whisper. " 'Much pain,' they kept repeating. 'But in the end, great lightness of being.' "

Meaning that if I starve now, I'll be thin later, Jupe thought. He felt the people on either side of him swinging slightly from side to side. A couple of voices in the group began to hum.

"Think of the hinges . . . slowly . . . opening . . ." Lovell intoned.

Pete imagined opening the door of his Toyota Corolla. How long was that Pitman arm going to take?

"There . . ." Lovell said. "Can you feel a strange new aura, like a sudden shifting of wind?"

This time, when another actor giggled, he was cut off by a loud "Shhh!"

Jupiter recognized that the *shhh* was not from Lovell. Some other cast member was annoyed. The group was getting into the spirit.

"Now . . . gently sway to your inner rhythms . . ."

Lovell said. "When we are swaying in sync, there will be a confluence of aura energy, and the visitor will be drawn out . . ."

Jupiter began to swing too. Keep cool, he said to himself. It's the power of suggestion, that's all. That's all . . .

"Yes . . ." Lovell whispered, his voice choked with excitement. "I believe it is here . . . I believe one of you feels it . . . *yes!*"

The next moment it was pitch-dark. But different from the darkness of closed eyes—sudden, inky black. The lamp had gone out.

"YEEAGHHH!" A scream pierced the silence. Jupiter jumped as a dull thud sounded against the carpet.

His eyes sprang open. "Get the light!" he called out.

There was a scramble of bodies in the darkness, a scratching of nails against the wall. In seconds an overhead light came on.

Kelly immediately gasped and grabbed Pete's arm.

"What the—?" Pete whispered.

Lying flat on his back, an ugly red mark above his closed eyes, was George.

Next to his head lay the marble bust of William Shakespeare.

6

Curtains?

"NO . . . NO, REALLY. I'M ALL RIGHT," GEORGE IN-sisted. He pushed away the cold, damp cloth that Lovell was trying to place on his forehead. The blow from the bust hadn't drawn blood, but there was a nasty bruise.

"I'll call the hospital," Pete said, reaching for the phone.

"*No!*" George replied. The force of his voice stopped Pete cold.

George looked from Pete to Jupiter. "I can't miss the show tonight—not after what happened this after-noon!"

Jupiter thought of the argument with Firestone and Crocker, and he understood George's fear. The actor was afraid of being fired. Before anyone could ask what George meant, Jupiter changed the subject. "How did this happen—did you trip against the ta-ble?"

George rubbed his sore forehead. "No. I was just sitting there with my eyes closed, and *wham!*"

"This thing is heavy," Kelly remarked, lifting the bust back onto the table.

"My mother always said I was hardheaded." George tried to laugh.

"Was it sitting on the edge of the table?" one of the other actors asked. "Maybe the vibrations in the room—"

Jupiter examined the top of the small table. "There's a raised edge around this," he said. "It couldn't have just slid off."

"Maybe we shouldn't have let that spirit come through the door," Vic said.

A weak ripple of laughter went through the room.

But Lovell Madeira didn't appear to find the joke funny. His eyes had a mysterious intensity as he looked at George. When he spoke, his voice was full of hidden meaning. "You know very well why this happened."

George returned a baffled, almost frightened glance. He laughed nervously and turned away.

"What are you talking about, Lovell?" one of the other actors asked.

Yes, what *is* he talking about? Jupe wondered. I'll have to ask George if I can ever get him alone.

Lovell looked at his watch. "Perhaps we'd better continue this another day. If we go now, we can get a bite before half-hour."

"That's a good idea," George said, rising to his feet. He turned down a half-dozen offers of aid as he walked slowly to the door.

The other theater people followed him, but Jupiter stayed behind with Pete and Kelly. "Mind if we look around a little?" he asked Lovell.

With his bag hooked over his shoulder, Lovell stood by the light switch and shook his head no. "It's very important we leave now," he said. "We've had a visitation by a very strong presence, and the aura of this room must be restored."

"But we just want to—"

Before Jupe could finish, Lovell clicked the light off.

They all trudged back through the hallway. There was no way Pete and Jupe could insist on staying without causing suspicion.

Jupiter gritted his teeth in frustration. The investigation had been put on hold before it even began.

◆　◆　◆

Jupiter's stomach growled as he walked through the stage door at seven thirty.

"I heard that," Pete said. "It's what you get for embarrassing us at the Burger Bistro."

"What else could I have done?" Jupiter retorted. "Red meat is not on my diet!"

Pete shook his head. "But you could have just *asked* for lettuce and tomatoes instead of saying, 'One Bistroburg Platter, hold the mayo, hold the pickle, hold the fries, hold the bun, hold the beef'!"

Jupiter shrugged. "I figured I'd talk to them in their own language."

George laughed. "Come on, I've got the house-seat order in my room."

George stopped to put a check mark next to his name on the sign-in sheet on the wall.

"We've got to sign in by a half-hour before the show," he explained. "If we're not here on time, Jim Bernardi gets the understudy ready."

Kelly noticed a new sign posted on the message board. "Hey, you didn't tell us about this, George!" The sign read:

For immediate release to trade newspapers:

*   <u>DANGER ZONE</u> CHORUS AUDITIONS   *

MAIN STAGE, GARBER THEATER

THURSDAY, 11:00 A.M.

AVAILABLE: ONE FEMALE PART, ONE MALE PART

"Why? Are you interested?" George asked.

Kelly's face began to turn red. "Well . . . yeah! I mean, I used to take dance lessons."

"Well, today's Tuesday, so you've got two days to prepare!" George said, winking at Kelly. He turned and led the others down the corridor, giving a wave to Luther in his office.

When the four of them got to George's dressing room, George picked up an envelope and handed it to Jupiter. "Okay, here they are. Best three seats in the house, fifth row center!" He let out a sudden whoop and spun around. "I can't believe this—I'm actually nervous that you guys are going to be out there!"

"Don't worry," Pete said. "We'll close our eyes every time you come on."

George pretended to push them out. "Hey, get out of here! I must prepare!"

Laughing, they left the dressing room. As they made their way to the front of the theater, Kelly said, "Wow, is he full of energy! I guess he's really up for the show. And that's after being conked on the head."

Pete nodded in agreement. "You know, I never thought about the theater before, but being backstage makes you feel so . . . juiced up. Like you can do whatever you want."

Jupiter couldn't help but feel a little pang of envy for George. Pete was right. It *was* a powerful feeling.

He hated to admit it to himself, but for the first time, he was beginning to regret giving up a life in show business.

◆   ◆   ◆

When the lights went out at the end of the show, there was a total silence. George's final number had been stunning. The last echoes of his strong voice were still floating through the theater.

The applause started slowly, a few timid claps. Then a sudden thunderous wave swept through the audience. In seconds everyone in the theater was standing and cheering.

"He was *incredible!*" Pete exclaimed. He put his fingers to his mouth and let out a loud whistle.

The stage lights came on and the chorus took a

curtain call. Then they backed away, leaving a space in the center for the lead actors to come through.

As the star of the show, George was the last to come out for his bow. The applause became a deafening roar as he stepped to the front of the stage. He smiled and bowed deeply. The bruise on his forehead was invisible under his makeup. He looked out to Jupiter, Pete, and Kelly and gave a little wink. Then he turned to hold hands with his costars.

"YEEE-HAAA—" Pete began.

He was cut off by an explosion of blinding light. The applause gave way to scattered shrieks and murmurs of surprise.

Jupiter gasped. Where George had been standing there was nothing but billowing smoke!

7

The Bard's Revenge

PETE, JUPITER, AND KELLY RUSHED TOWARD THE AISLE, squeezing past confused audience members who were rising out of their seats.

"Coming through!" Pete shouted as he cleared a path through the people clogging the aisles. Jupiter and Kelly followed him past the orchestra pit and up onto the stage.

The smoke had cleared. George lay motionless on the stage floor, surrounded by cast members. Pete and Jupiter elbowed their way to him. "Give him some breathing room!" Jupiter ordered.

Some of the others backed away as Jupiter knelt beside George. An actress was cradling his head. "Is he all right?" Jupiter asked, leaning close to George's face to listen for breathing. Jupiter noticed a faint red mark on his forehead.

"Kiss my forehead," came a breathless whisper.

Jupiter sprang back. "Huh?"

"They . . . they have to carry me offstage. . . . Where's the orchestra?"

"George! It's Jupiter Jones! Are you all right?"

George's eyes blinked open. "J-Jupiter! I must have passed out. I thought I was doing the death scene from *West Side Story*."

Jupiter noticed some of the cast members smiling with relief. But it was clear from George's dazed expression that he wasn't joking.

Jim Bernardi and a tall, strapping dancer helped George stand up.

"I'm okay, really," George protested as he staggered offstage with them.

The audience members who had stayed behind gave a smattering of applause. As the onlookers began to file out, Jupiter peered over the edge of the stage.

In the orchestra pit a couple of electricians were examining wires that led to a metal device attached to the edge of the stage. Buzz Newman and another musician stood around watching.

Jupiter nodded a greeting. "What happened?"

Buzz shrugged. "Wish I knew. It nearly took my head off."

"Loose connection to the flash-pot," a craggy-faced electrician said. He looked up into Pete's blank expression. "That's this little container here. It has a very weak explosive that sends off smoke when it's ignited by an electrical signal." He looked at the blackened box and shrugged. "Could have been a power surge that sent a stray signal."

"Does that happen very often?" Jupiter asked.

"First time I've seen it," the man replied. "But it's possible."

Possible, but not likely, Jupiter thought.

He and Pete watched the electrician for a few seconds, then walked back to George's dressing room. There Kelly and a few of the cast members were talking and making tea in an electric hot pot. George sat at his makeup table, his phone receiver propped on his shoulder. "A flash-pot," he said into the phone. "I don't know *how* it went off. . . . As I was taking a curtain call. . . . Aren't you going to ask how I am? . . . Yeah, I'm okay, Ruthie. . . . Yeah, see you."

As he hung up, he sank back in his seat and said, "Hi, Jupe." Then he called out to the other actors, "Listen, you guys, thanks a lot for helping me out, but I—I have these guests here . . ."

The actors cheerfully nodded and left the room. George shivered slightly. His eyes seemed to grow hollow and more distant by the second. "Three accidents in one night," he said, gingerly touching his forehead. "I don't know how much more of this I can take before . . ." His voice trailed off.

Jupiter leaned forward. "Why don't you start by telling me what you know about everyone associated with the show."

Jupiter noticed George's eyes rising upward, looking past him. He turned to see Lovell Madeira standing in the doorway.

"Thank goodness you're all right," Lovell said.

George gave a halfhearted smirk. "Why, Lovell? Did old Will take it easy on me? Maybe I should stop saying 'Macbeth,' huh?"

Lovell stiffened. "You haven't learned your lesson, have you?"

"Let me clue you in," George said, turning to Jupiter, Pete, and Kelly. "I'm not supposed to say 'Macbeth.' If I say that word, I'll be zapped by the Macbeth curse."

Each time he said the word "Macbeth," Lovell's expression got more sour. "Stop it, George!"

"What's going on?" Pete asked.

Lovell shook his head sadly. "It's the oldest theatrical curse in the world. The name of Shakespeare's Scottish play must never be mentioned backstage. Any actor who does so will be visited by great misfortune—"

"The play he's talking about is *Macbeth*," George cut in.

Lovell's nostrils flared. "People have died mocking the curse! And don't think you'll be the exception to the rule. You think it's an *accident* that all these things are going wrong?" He turned away, then looked over his shoulder. "Take the advice of a friend. Be a rebel if you want to, but watch out. The spirit of William Shakespeare is not known to be forgiving!"

He cocked his chin high in the air and marched into the hallway.

Pete gave Jupe a significant look.

Softly George mimicked a trumpet fanfare. "What a flake," he said. "I love to get him going on that old theater stuff."

Jupiter seemed lost in thought.

After a minute Pete said, "He may not be so far off base. It sure isn't working your way."

George rolled his eyes. "Now he's got *you* hooked on this mumbo jumbo!" He looked from one to the other, then grumpily folded his arms. "Okay, you guys are the experts. I'll try to stop teasing Lovell."

"All right," Jupiter said, changing the subject, "let's start talking about who's in the show."

◆   ◆   ◆

They left the theater an hour later, George in his car and Jupiter with Pete and Kelly in the pickup. Jupiter had listened carefully as George filled them in on the theater people. But nothing seemed any clearer.

Jupiter followed George, making sure he got safely home. Kelly had to be awakened when they finally reached her house. Jupe dropped her off and headed with Pete to The Three Investigators' headquarters.

Headquarters was on the outskirts of Rocky Beach. There Jupiter's Aunt Mathilda and Uncle Titus had set up The Jones Salvage Yard, the area's most unusual junkyard. Over the years they'd collected both useful and exotic artifacts—everything from toasters to rare books.

As Jupiter and Pete passed through wrought-iron entrance gates (salvaged by Uncle Titus from an old estate), their minds jumped back to the case.

"I think it's Bernardi," Pete said. "He calls the shots backstage. He could have caused the flash-pot explosion."

"True," Jupiter answered. "But he wasn't at Lovell Madeira's house. He couldn't have been the one who cut the lights and toppled the Shakespeare bust onto George. And what about the falling sign?"

He came to a stop by Headquarters, an old mobile-home trailer with an addition that Jupiter had built himself. It was a gray, run-down shack, but the satellite dish on its roof gave a hint at what was inside—a full electronics workshop, complete with a camcorder, closed-circuit TV, infrared devices, and voice-activated tape recorders.

"Besides," Jupiter continued, getting out of the pickup, "where's the motive? What does Bernardi have against George?"

Pete shrugged as they stepped into the workshop. "Beats me. It's just a hunch I have. Who do you think did it—that Bruno guy?"

"Well, he was there when the sign fell, *and* he works backstage—but George just told us he only handles set pieces, not electrical equipment." Jupiter plopped down on a sofa against the wall and turned on the TV news with the remote control. "Of course, he could easily be mad at George for *something*. I think he's mad at the world."

Pete settled into the opposite end of the sofa. "You know, the flash-pot was in the orchestra pit. Maybe it wasn't set off by an electrician. Maybe a musician did it."

"Like Buzz Newman?"

Pete nodded. "I wouldn't count Lovell out either. You never know what a weirdo like that might be up to. Not to mention Vic Hammil. He was in Lovell's apartment, and if anything ever happened to George, guess who would be the new star of the show?"

"Maybe not Vic," Jupiter countered. "Manny Firestone would probably hire Matt Grant right away. I'm not sure we can count Firestone out of this."

Instead of answering, Pete sat bolt upright. "Hey, look at this!"

An image of the Garber Theater had come onto the TV screen. The camera panned slowly back to reveal Jewel Coleman beginning to interview George that afternoon. Her voice was barely audible, drowned out by an offscreen voice that said, "In tonight's final news item, more bizarre incidents involving the show *Danger Zone* occurred today. Late this afternoon, star George Brandon barely escaped severe injury when a massive sign tore loose from a crane above him."

The camera cut to a panic-stricken Bruno, shouting

a warning. Then it cut to a slow-motion image of the sign tumbling toward the sidewalk. Below it, everyone scrambled for cover.

Pete cringed as the sign crashed to the ground. The next thing to fill the screen was George's sweaty, shocked face, stammering into Jewel's mike.

Then came a description of the flash-pot explosion and George's injury at the channeling session.

"How did the newspeople find out about those events?" Jupe said.

"Are all these accidents, or are they the work of something a little more . . . unusual?" the voice went on. "*Late-Night News* spoke to several people, one of whom believes there is a higher, more dangerous force at work."

Lovell Madeira appeared. Standing outside the theater, he stared nervously into the camera and told about the Macbeth curse and George's flouting of it.

When Lovell finished, the reporter turned to the camera. With a grim expression he said, "It's common knowledge in the theater world that the real name of the so-called Scottish play is never *ever* mentioned backstage. Is it superstition? Some say yes, but even they stop short of actually calling the play by name. More than three hundred and fifty years after the death of the Bard of Avon, we may be discovering why the tradition still holds strong. As a frightened George Brandon would tell you, the price of breaking the taboo may be very, very high."

Pete turned to Jupe. "Who's the Bard of Avon?"

"It's a nickname for William Shakespeare."

Pete looked uneasy. "Uh, Jupe, I know you don't believe in any of this stuff, but there's your answer."

"What do you mean?"

"It isn't Buzz or Lovell or any of those guys who's out to get George. It's Shakespeare's ghost!"

8

Behind the Scenes

BOB WAS WIDE-EYED THE NEXT MORNING WHEN JUPITER told him what had happened. "Bummer! Now I wish I'd been with you guys last night," he said. "This new band I saw was a real washout."

Jupiter turned from Bob and flipped on his computer. "Well, I know you're busy this week, but try to keep an ear open for any clues."

"I'll talk to Buzz about it. He's supposed to come by any minute."

Jupiter spun around. "He's coming *here*?"

"Yeah," Bob said, a little defensive at Jupiter's tone of voice. "He's a fanatic about sound systems. When I told him we had quadraphonic speakers here, he wanted to bring over some tapes."

"Did you tell him who we are?"

"No. I just said we hung out here, that's all. Did I blow something?"

"No, not at all. Just make sure you keep our identities as the Three Investigators a secret. We haven't ruled out anyone in this case—including Buzz."

He wheeled around on his swivel chair to face the computer. It was one of the three that usually sat in the air-conditioned HQ trailer. He'd moved this one into his workshop for convenience.

With a few quick flicks of his fingers Jupe logged on to the DataServe network, an information service that contained a complete encyclopedia.

"Hey!" came a voice from the entrance. "Anybody home? Do I need a secret password?"

Bob shot Jupiter a quick look, then called out, "Come on in, Buzz!"

Buzz stepped in, carrying a canvas shoulder bag. He looked around the workshop, grinning broadly. "Wh-o-oa, nice digs! What do I have to do to join the club?"

Bob laughed. "We'll talk about that after we see what kind of tapes you brought." He reached into Buzz's bag and took out a handful of cassettes. "Ugh! *The Most Happy Fella, West Side Story, Candide, Sweeney Todd*—it's all show music! What did you do, take your father's collection by mistake?"

"No, man!" Buzz said. "I've really been getting into this stuff lately."

Bob shook his head. "I thought you were a rock musician! This music is so . . . *shallow* compared to the good stuff."

"I know where you're coming from. I didn't go for it much either till I started hanging out with George Brandon. I swear that dude knows every song from every musical ever written. A lot of it is garbage, but some of it's more hip than you think!"

Bob looked at him warily. "And I thought you were playing *Danger Zone* just to make some money. Looks to me like you're really selling out."

"Hey, chill out! I have to make some bucks, man. Playing a long-running show is the best steady gig you can get—*you* know that. Why shouldn't I at least try to get into the music?"

Bob sighed and sank into a chair. "Okay, but from what I hear, the show-biz life isn't much better than the rock scene. If the show closes, you lose your job. Besides, let's face it, the big money is in rock—for those who make it."

"Yeah," Buzz said, "for those *few* who make it." He went over to a cassette player and stuck in the tape marked *Sweeney Todd*. "Now here's some great show music. Listen to this!"

Eerie, fast-paced music resounded through the workshop. Jupiter liked it. It put him in the right mood for looking up information about the Macbeth curse. His fingers flew over the keyboard: THEATER . . . SUPERSTITION . . . CURSES . . .

He scanned them all and found nothing.

MACBETH . . .

The screen showed a summary of the play, all about a man named Macbeth who commits a murder to become king. Witches warn that he will die when the woods around the castle close in on him. The warning comes true—but the "woods" are actually soldiers holding cut tree branches as camouflage. Macbeth dies in a bloody revolt.

Jupiter scrolled past some background historical information. Then came a list of four movies that had been made of the story.

Suddenly Jupiter stopped reading. *Woods closing in . . .* why did that sound familiar?

The ringing of the workshop phone startled Jupe. He reached for it, but Bob was already there.

The phone! What were those crank phone messages and letters George had gotten?

Jupiter pulled his case notes out of a file cabinet drawer and scanned the first page. Right away he saw what he wanted.

> —*British accent, old-person's voice saying 'Beware, thespian!'*
> —*letters saying he's going to die in a throne of blood*
> —*letter: something about a forest moving in to swallow him up*

Jupe sat back in his chair. The threats *had* to refer to *Macbeth*. And almost certainly they referred to the Macbeth curse—the curse that George loved to flout.

Jupe pondered. Could Lovell have done the voice, written the letters? Would he go to all that trouble just to prove the curse was true? And if he did, was he also responsible for the attempts on George's life? What would he gain?

Or maybe someone was setting Lovell up—someone who knew how upset Lovell was about the curse.

A nagging, chilly feeling hit Jupiter. Was it possible that the curse was true?

He tried to laugh that one off. *Pete* was the one who believed in ghosts, not him.

But still . . .

Bob's voice invaded his thoughts. "That was Pete on the phone, Jupe. He told me to tell you he was going over to school for a while to watch Kelly at cheerleading practice."

"Thanks," Jupiter said absently.

"All right, enough of this stuff," Bob said to Buzz as the tape ended. "How about some lunch at Taco 'Round the Clock—my treat!"

"Hey, you're talking my language," said Buzz.

"How about you, Jupe?" Bob asked.

At the thought of tacos Jupiter felt his taste buds tingle. But he'd gone too far on his diet to back off now. His Hawaiian Bermuda shorts were beginning to loosen up around the waist. "No, thanks," he answered. "I've got more research. And then I'm scheduled to get together with Pete. George invited us to come watch him rehearse a new dance number."

"Then I'll see you later," said Buzz as Bob led him out of the workshop.

Jupiter tried to keep his mind on the screen. But now all he could think about was the food he had turned down the last couple of days: a juicy bacon cheeseburger at Bud's Healthworks, a steaming taco plate, those moist sticky buns . . . A vivid image popped into his head—an image of George and Vic biting into the sticky buns in front of Lovell's apartment—

Lovell's apartment.

"Hmmm," Jupiter muttered. Some business had been left unfinished yesterday, some business that might be very revealing . . .

Kicking the chair back, he made for the door. Saved from carbohydrates one more time. Now if only Lovell Madeira was still home.

9

A Sticky Point

FIRST STOP WAS ROCKY BEACH HIGH SCHOOL. AS JUPITER parked his pickup near the football field, he scanned the bleachers for Pete.

It wasn't hard to find him. He was sitting alone in the front row, practically the only male there.

The cheerleaders' voices rang through the warm, early afternoon air:

"Ou-r guys are outta sight!
Rocky Beach is DY-NO-MITE!"

No competition for Shakespeare, Jupiter thought as he stepped into the bleachers. Pete was leaning back, elbows on the bench behind him. He smiled at Jupiter. "I had a feeling you'd come. They've got some hot-looking new members on the squad."

"Oh." Jupiter took a quick look at the field, where Kelly was leading a group of girls in a cheer. Pete was right. Not that it meant anything. The prettier the girl, the more awkward Jupiter felt. Just *thinking* about girls put a knot in his throat.

But Jupe's job right now was *unraveling* knots, not making new ones. "That's not the reason I'm here," he said. "I have an idea—and it means going to Lovell Madeira's apartment before the rehearsal. But first I need to ask Kelly a question."

Pete looked over Jupiter's shoulder. "Better catch her now. Looks like they're taking a break."

Jupiter stood up and stepped onto the small patch of grass in front of the bleachers. He noticed that his action caught the eyes of a couple of girls.

Immediately he felt as if his legs had grown to the size of tree trunks. He could feel every strain his stomach put on his shirt buttons. His foot suddenly caught on the lip of the rubberized asphalt track that surrounded the football field. He stumbled, his feet slapping the ground to prevent his fall.

"Ooof!" He let the startled breath out of his mouth. The two pretty girls exchanged a half-smile and turned away.

Jupiter was mortified. In an instant they had sized him up and blotted him out of their minds. And what had happened to *him* in that same tiny sliver of time? Utter, unspeakable, crawl-in-a-hole-and-die humiliation!

No—he couldn't give in to that feeling. Not when there was a mystery that needed his superior skills. If there was a time to rely on his acting experience, it was now. Jupiter pulled himself up and sauntered onto the field with a walk that oozed confidence.

"Jupiter, are you all right? You look a little weird," Kelly said.

At least he *thought* he oozed confidence. "No, I'm fine. I need to talk to you—alone."

"Okay." She took him over to the fence, out of earshot from the others. "I have to be back in five minutes. We're trying to get a new cheer ready for the first day of school."

"I just need to know one thing. In Lovell Madeira's apartment yesterday, you picked up the bust of Shakespeare that fell on George. Do you remember what it felt like?"

Kelly hesitated. "Like . . . like *marble*, I guess. Cool, smooth—"

"I mean, was there anything on it—a stain of some sort?"

Kelly thought for a moment. "Well, now that you mention it, I remember it *was* sort of sticky."

"What kind of stickiness?" Jupiter asked, trying to contain his excitement. "Like glue? Like food?"

"I didn't really notice. I—"

She was cut off by Pete's voice. "Hey, can three play?"

They turned to see Pete approaching. "Pete," Jupiter said, "your girlfriend has the earmarks of a great detective."

"I could have told you that," Kelly said. "Uh, what did I say?"

"I'm not sure yet." Jupe glanced up at the stadium

clock, which read 1:05. "We have less than an hour to visit Lovell. We've got to be back at the theater by two. That's when rehearsal starts for that new dance number. I have a hunch that—"

"Wait a minute," Kelly interrupted. "Did you say *we*?"

"Well, yes," Jupiter said, surprised at her stern tone of voice. "Pete and I. You would be welcome, but you have practice."

Instead of answering, Kelly shot a look at Pete.

Pete shifted uncomfortably from side to side. "Uh, yeah . . . you see, Jupe, Kelly's gonna do a new cheer, one that she made up herself, and I'm supposed to—I mean, I really *want* to see it."

Kelly smiled, and Jupiter immediately realized he was on his own. For a second he felt irritated. Was he the *only* Investigator who was serious about this case? But then he remembered all the times Bob and Pete *had* been there.

"Meet you at the theater at two o'clock?" Jupiter asked.

"Our rehearsal's over at one thirty," Kelly answered. "We'll both be there."

"Great. See you."

Jupiter trotted back to the parking lot, taking care to suck in his gut as he passed the cheerleaders. He couldn't blame Pete for being a social success—much. Jupe got into the pickup and sped toward the freeway, in the direction of West Hollywood.

He knew this wasn't going to be easy. As he drove, he tried to think of a way to get information out of Lovell without revealing why he needed it.

His digital watch blinked exactly one thirty as he parked in front of Lovell's apartment. He ran up the cement pathway, rang the doorbell, and waited.

"Yes?" came a muffled voice from the other side of the door.

"Jupiter Jones."

The name was met by silence.

"George Brandon's friend!" Jupiter added.

The door swung open. "I didn't know your name was *Jupiter*," Lovell said, his eyes narrowed. "Jupiter, hmmm . . . I would say your personality was more *Saturnian*—inquisitive, a collector of information."

"Well, to tell you the truth," Jupiter said, suddenly feeling very uncomfortable, "I *did* come here to ask a few questions. Mind if I come in?"

Lovell looked at his watch. "I'll have to leave for the theater in a few minutes. What can I do for you?"

"Let me get right to the point, Mr. Madeira," Jupiter said with a concerned frown. "I'm worried about George. I think he's courting danger by mocking the curse. I'd like your advice about what I can do—as a friend."

With a solemn nod Lovell stepped back from the door. "Come in."

A look of triumph flickered across the man's face as he led Jupiter toward the room at the end of the corridor. "So, I take it you were intrigued by our session."

"Yes, I was. Although I have to admit my hunger threatened to overwhelm me at times."

Lovell chuckled. "Yes, these things are best done on an empty stomach. I hadn't eaten all day myself."

Jupiter made a mental note. Apparently George and Vic had kept all the sticky buns to themselves.

The room of astrological charts was tidy. Lovell flicked on the light switch, which was just to the right of the door. A little farther to the right was the wall outlet, with a long cord plugged into it. The middle section of the cord made several loops on the floor before extending up to the lamp, which sat on its table. Against the opposite wall stood the bust of Shakespeare on its table, frowning gloomily.

Jupiter estimated that the bust was about fifteen feet across the room from the lamp's outlet. He tried to review who had been sitting where on the Oriental rug, starting at the door and circling to the right: first Lovell, then a girl with glasses, a curly-haired guy, Vic, then three other cast members. George had been next, sitting closest to the bust, then two or three actresses. Jupiter, Pete, and Kelly had completed the circle up the left side.

Jupiter quickly decided on his line of attack. "The thing is, I still find it hard to believe it wasn't all some sort of a . . . a . . ."

"A trick?" Lovell finished, smiling placidly. "Yes, many first-timers have that reaction to a visitation. But I challenge you to tell me how that lamp could have gone out all by itself."

"I guess it could have been on a timer," Jupiter replied.

Lovell chuckled. "Yes, and then I hopped across the room over everyone in the dark, toppled the bust, and raced back to turn on the overhead light, right?"

"Well, maybe the bulb blew or something. Did you check it when you got home?"

"Naturally. The bulb was fine. The lamp's plug was out of the socket."

Bingo, Jupiter thought. I should have noticed that. I was too worried about George. "Someone may have pulled it," he suggested.

"Not someone," Lovell said ominously. "Some-thing."

Jupiter pretended to consider that statement deeply. "It *is* pretty bizarre . . ."

Lovell put an arm on Jupiter's shoulder. "Young man, you have a responsibility to your friend. He will certainly respect your opinion more than mine. Talk to him. *Warn* him." He glanced at his watch. "Now, I hate to be a rude host, but I've got to get to the theater. Rehearsals wait for no man."

"Yes, of course." Jupiter turned and walked back up the corridor. "By the way, my friend Kelly sends her apologies. You see, she had been eating some sticky buns before the session, and we came so late she didn't have time to wash her hands. In the confusion after the lights went out, she says she probably smeared her hands over some of your stuff."

Lovell thought a moment and nodded. "Yes, she was the one who picked up the bust, wasn't she? I *did* have to wash a rather sugary substance off it. Smelled sort of like cinnamon. I noticed it on the light switch, too."

Jupiter didn't let his surprise show. "Well, she's sorry."

Lovell smiled. "You tell her not to worry. I had it wiped off in a jiffy."

"Thanks."

The two of them walked out the front door. As Lovell locked it behind him, he said, "You'll have to join the group again sometime—although I believe I'll wait a while until Will calms down."

"Will?"

"Shakespeare, of course."

"Oh, right," Jupiter said. "Well, see you at the theater."

He climbed back into the pickup and drove onto the freeway. Before long his speedometer read fifty-five, but his brain was doing one hundred. It was clear now—*Vic* was the culprit. He was the only one besides George who was eating those sticky buns. Could *he* have pulled the plug, gone across the room, toppled the bust, then gone back across the room to turn on the light switch—in the dark?

Jupiter's brow furrowed. That was the same scenario

Lovell had mocked moments ago, when Jupiter had accused him. But Vic was younger and quicker than Lovell. It wasn't impossible.

Jupiter was sure of only one thing. The culprit wasn't the ghost of William Shakespeare.

Unless the ghost ate sticky buns.

10

Stage Struck

JUPITER SLOWED TO A STOP BEFORE DRIVING INTO THE Garber Theater parking lot. A line of people parted to let him through. His eyes followed the line to the right. It snaked along the fer.ce almost a full block to the theater box office.

They must have all seen the news last night, Jupiter thought. Amazing what a near tragedy could do for business—even in previews.

He drove in, passing over a set of frightening-looking metal spikes that pointed sharply into the lot. They were mounted on spring hinges that allowed the spikes to sink into the ground as long as you were driving *in*. If you drove *out*—instead of using the exit and paying your fee—your tires became a mass of shredded rubber. Even though these devices were fairly common in Southern California, they reminded Jupiter of medieval torture chambers.

There were two dull clanks as the spikes sprang back up after each set of wheels passed over them. Jupiter parked and ran inside the theater's stage door.

Luther nodded to him as he walked through the corridor, past the corkboard. Just inside the door to the stage, Pete was already talking to George. Jupiter could see no sign of the bruise on George's forehead.

"Greetings," Jupiter said. "I see you survived the night."

George rapped his knuckles lightly on a props table. "Knock on wood, nothing has happened since I saw you."

Jupiter looked around. "I thought Kelly was coming."

"She's over there," Pete said, gesturing with his head toward a dimly lit corner.

There, Kelly was quietly tracing a few easy jazz-dance steps on the floor. Her long brown hair gently bobbed up and down.

"What's she doing?" Jupiter asked.

Pete smiled. "Remember that sign in the corridor?"

"You mean the audition notice? Has she decided to—?"

"Who knows?" Pete said with a shrug. "I think she's just dreaming."

"*Places for 'Kyoto con Moto'!*" Jim Bernardi's voice crackled over the backstage loudspeakers.

"That's the big dance number we're putting in tonight," George said. "Why don't you guys watch it from the house?"

"That means the audience," Jupiter explained to Pete, relieving his puzzled expression.

They got Kelly's attention, and then all three walked through a side door into the audience.

As soon as they sat down, the stage went dark. A motor rumbled and then a piano started to play soft, Oriental-sounding music from inside the orchestra pit.

"Where are the other musicians?" Pete whispered.

"Too expensive to have them around for all the rehearsals," Jupiter answered.

Various lights went on, illuminating a set of huge, translucent Japanese screens from behind. It was a quiet, simple effect, but there was something ominous about it.

Suddenly the music became loud and pulsating, with a strong rock beat. Dancers flashed across the stage, behind the screen. Only their shadows were visible. As they crisscrossed, they seemed to pass through one another. Their sharp, angular movements combined martial arts technique with jazz dance.

Jupiter was fascinated. Thin, bright ribbons of laser light now sliced the air in front of the screens.

Suddenly all the dancers turned upstage and froze in position. Behind the center screen a dancer leaped onto the stage, seeming to fly through the air. His shadow landed gracefully and began a dazzling solo.

"That's George!" Kelly said, amazed.

Jupiter watched the shadow. He knew George was a good dancer, but he'd never seen him do anything like this. The shadow commanded the stage, slicing and kicking with sharp precision.

"He's not bad," Pete remarked. "I mean, in terms of the martial arts."

Jupiter could sense a little "I can do that" in Pete's voice. Now George's shadow was climbing a tall structure at the rear of the stage. He stood on it, his hands thrust outward. The dancers below him started moving furiously. Then, slowly bending his knees, he sprang from the structure with a dazzling leap that seemed to suspend him in midair forever.

And that's when the rumbling began again.

Jupiter's eyes widened. "The turntable!"

George's shadow was looking straight ahead. A safe landing depended on the floor being stationary beneath him. If he didn't know the turntable was moving . . .

The screens shook. Dancers fell to the floor, crying out in surprise. Loud voices erupted backstage.

And when George's shadow landed with a loud thud, his legs buckled beneath him. Screaming with pain, he crumbled to the floor like a rag doll.

Jupiter, Pete, and Kelly leaped out of their seats and ran onstage. The music stopped, the house lights went on, and the stage swarmed with people.

But their approach was abruptly stopped by a strong tattooed arm. "No unauthorized people onstage," a gravelly voice informed them.

It was Bruno. He glowered at the three of them, saving his angriest look for Jupiter.

"But you know us!" Jupiter pleaded as Bruno ushered them into the wings.

Bruno nodded. "No kidding. I also know that only cast and personnel are allowed on the stage—especially in situations like this." He shrugged. "Liability insurance reasons—the company can't be responsible for you if something happens."

Jupiter looked back at the stage helplessly. Bruno's statement made sense. He wasn't just getting even.

"Some help we are," Pete muttered.

"What's going on? The set fall apart or something?" Jupiter spun around at the familiar voice.

In unison he, Pete, and Kelly blurted out "George!"

On two sure, steady legs, George sauntered toward them. "Tune it up a little. You guys have potential." He peered past them onto the stage. "Is anybody going to tell me what's going on?"

"B-but that was *you*," Kelly sputtered, pointing into the center of the commotion.

Jim Bernardi and a stagehand were now lifting someone off the stage. Someone as tall as George with sandy blond hair and a freckled face.

"No, it wasn't," Jupiter said softly. "But the shadow was the same."

"You see," Pete explained, "we thought . . . from out there . . ." He gestured toward the house.

George's puzzled expression suddenly cleared. "Oh, I get it. John Warren had an accident onstage, and you thought it was me because you only saw the shadow!"

"Right!" Kelly exclaimed.

"It makes sense," George said. "He's *supposed* to

look like me. He was hired to do that number because I can't do those moves . . ." His voice trailed off.

A voice could be heard shouting "Hank! What happened with the turntable?"

Tointable. Jupiter couldn't help but notice again Jim Bernardi's New York accent.

From stage right a voice answered back, "You gave cue seventy-seven, right? That's a turntable cue!"

"What!" Bernardi glanced with alarm at the computer stand, but his hands were full getting the dancer off the stage.

"Maybe something's wrong with the computer!" the turntable operator bellowed.

Jupiter could hear Bernardi mutter "Brilliant deduction" as he set John Warren down on a backstage cot and ran to the phone.

George went up to John and asked, "You all right?"

His voice pinched with pain, John answered, "I think I broke my ankle."

As George knelt by John's cot, keeping him company, Pete turned to Jupiter and Kelly. "Poor guy. That'll take forever to heal. He'll be out for months."

But Jupiter was preoccupied. "We're in trouble. What if that *had* been George? If we're not allowed onstage, we might as well be handcuffed."

"What can we do?" Pete asked. "We're not stagehands. We're not in the show. And we can't pretend to be—everybody knows our faces now." He exhaled. "It's hopeless."

"Unless . . ." Kelly said, her eyes glittering. Jupiter

and Pete followed her glance as she looked toward the outer corridor.

The audition notice was visible through the half-open door. It flapped lightly as a breeze blew in from outside.

Pete guffawed. "Just can't get your mind off that, can you? Come on, be serious."

"No," Jupiter said, feeling a rush of excitement. "She's right, Pete! What an idea! There's one female and one male part available."

Kelly corrected him. "*Two* male parts, now. One for a tall, handsome young guy who specializes in martial arts. Someone like—"

Both Kelly and Jupiter looked at Pete.

"What . . . ? Who—me?" Pete began backing away. "Oh, no. I know what you two nutcases are thinking. No way, José! I'm not going anywhere near that audition. I've never been on a stage in my life— and I like it that way!"

"You're perfect for that part, Pete!" Jupiter urged. "You *know* you can do those moves! And I'll try out for the other male part."

"That's easy for you to say, Jupe. You were the big child star! And Kelly, you at least *want* to be in the theater. You two can audition your heads off if you want to. But me?" Pete shrugged defensively. "I'm 0 for two—no training, no desire. Besides, I'd get nervous."

"Nervous?" Jupiter said. "You've been on a football field and a basketball court. You've remained cool and calm during the wild applause of adoring fans. This is no different."

"Peter Dunstan Crenshaw!" Kelly's voice was firm. "This is the opportunity of a lifetime. We could share a wonderful new experience. And you would be doing the most you could to solve your case. Besides, Jupe can give you pointers on stage technique."

Pete's eyes darted from Kelly to Jupiter like a trapped animal's. He swallowed. "Y-you can?"

A broad, confident smile broke across Jupiter's face. "Pete, my boy, I'll make you a star!"

11

Facing the Music

"Kick, step, step, turn! Chassé left, chassé right. Hip, hip, arm, arm! Now *leap!*"

Pete felt the sweat drip off his brow like water breaking over a dam. He tried to follow the dance instructor's commands, but it was harder than doing a complex basketball pattern.

It was several hours after the accident at the Garber Theater. Jupe had dragged Pete off to a dance studio to practice for tomorrow's audition.

It's all for the case, Pete kept chanting to himself over and over again. *It may save George's life.* How come *Bob* wasn't being pressured into auditioning? Then he remembered Bob's demanding work schedule—lucky stiff!

He looked at Jupiter, who had walked over to the side, barely avoiding the arms and legs of the other class members. Leaning against the wooden bar that ran across the wall, Jupiter massaged his thigh. His face was beet red, his hair black with sweat. Albert

Einstein's face on Jupiter's T-shirt looked wrinkled and distorted as it clung to his drenched torso.

"If you can do judo, jazz dance is a piece of cake." Those were Jupiter's exact words, Pete remembered. But for someone who showed decent form in judo class, Jupiter looked pretty hopeless as a dancer. And he was supposed to be showing *Pete* the ropes.

"Okay, good work!" the instructor shouted. "Now let's warm down with some stretches. Ready? Demi-plié . . . plié . . . relevé . . . up, up, up! Arms rounded!"

Pete's calves strained as he stood on tiptoe. Out of the corner of his eye he saw Jupiter struggling to keep his balance. Jupiter blinked wildly, trying to fend off rivulets of salty sweat that were pouring into his eyes.

With a desperate wobble, followed by a resounding *whump*, Jupiter landed on the floor.

Pete closed his eyes. They were *both* going to be humiliated at this audition tomorrow. How had he ever let himself get talked into this?

◆　　　◆　　　◆

The next day Pete felt as if he had been run over by a truck. To add to his pain, he had to wait for the audition to begin along with dozens of perfect-looking dancers. Each was dressed in a stylish, expensive outfit that made Pete's gray sweatpants and Schmertz Auto Parts T-shirt seem crude by comparison. As he stared, one dancer leaped so high off the floor that his head grazed the ceiling. Another spun three times in a graceful blur. Still another stretched into a perfect split that Pete found excruciating to watch.

"These guys aren't human, Jupe," Pete said under his breath. "Not only aren't they sweating—*they're talking while they're doing it!* I can't even walk without feeling like a gorilla here!"

With a confident smile Jupiter bent to touch his toes. His fingertips barely cleared his knees. He slowly straightened and said, "Don't worry. They don't know the secret."

"Yeah? Well, could you let *me* in on it?"

"The secret is charisma," Jupe said.

"Great. Where do I buy some?"

Jupe ignored him and kept going. "They're not looking for perfection. They're looking for someone who takes control of the stage. You give the director the message that *you're* the guy for this part and he'd be a fool not to snap you up."

"How do you know all this, anyway?" Pete said. "You never even auditioned for *The Wee Rogues!*"

"True, but the director always used to let me watch whenever he held auditions for the other roles. And there's one thing I'll never forget, Pete—ninety percent of the time the part was cast the minute the right person walked onto the stage."

"But what if you really stink? Doesn't that count for anything?"

Jupiter wrapped his sweaty arm around Pete's shoulder. "In the last day, with my guidance, you've learned

more about movement and dance than most people
learn in years. You *don't* stink, Pete. You're an athlete
who's highly trained in martial arts, and your movements have natural grace. That's more than half the
battle. If they see that, they'll know they can train you
the rest of the way. You have one simple job today."
He looked his friend square in the eye. "Just show
them you can conquer the world."

Pete felt a surge of power. Sure, Jupiter's words were
corny, but they had the ring of truth. After all, if that
dumb Matt Grant could make it and threaten George's
job . . .

Pete pulled himself up to his full height. There
was a mission to be accomplished, a life to be saved.
And yes—he, Peter Crenshaw, was the man who
could do it! With a cocksure smile he strode through
the pack of whirling dancers to the stairwell that led
to stage level. Might as well be the first one up, he
thought.

There was a clatter of footsteps above him. The last
group of girls had finished auditioning, and Pete knew
Kelly was one of them. After a morning of auditions
and callbacks, this had been the final cut. Pete felt a
jolt of nerves.

Kelly bounced down with an enthusiastic smile.
She threw her arms around Pete.

"You made it!" he said.

She shook her head. "No such luck. But I made it
all the way to the second-to-last cut. Pretty darned
good!"

Pete smiled. "Congratulations."

"Thanks." Kelly gave him a kiss and continued down the stairs. "I'll wait for you. Break a leg!"

He looked at her, startled.

"Oh, that's what the actors all say to each other—it means 'good luck.' Bye!"

Alone again, Pete could feel his confidence eroding. If *Kelly* couldn't make it . . .

A bearded man in a T-shirt and tights appeared at the top of the stairs. "Okay, guys! Let's line up!"

Like a herd of cattle pressing through a narrow gate, the guys crowded together at the base of the stairs.

"I'm Ron deJomb, the choreographer. I hope you've all brushed up on your kung fu and tai chi. I'll teach the combination in groups, and then I'll see you one by one—where I'll *really* pick you apart!" He smiled.

There was weak laughter from the dancers. At the back of the crowd, Jupiter looked uneasy. Pete crossed his fingers. Maybe he *would* break a leg. Then he wouldn't have to go through this torture.

He began his silent chant again. *It's all for the case . . . It may save George's life. . . .*

◆　　　◆　　　◆

Kick, kick, leap. Right arm, left arm, spin, stop. The music ended.

There. That was it. The best Pete could do. He stood alone on the stage, his chest heaving.

"Just a second, Pete," deJomb called out from the audience.

Pete's stomach seemed to take on a life of its own.

It leaped and turned and fluttered. At least deJomb hadn't said "Thank you." Jupiter had warned him that those were the code words for "No, thank you." So far deJomb had been very hard to please. Every dancer had gotten a "thank you"—including Jupiter.

DeJomb was whispering animatedly with the show's director, Craig Jacobs. They kept looking at Pete. They were trying to decide something.

Pete began to feel dizzy. Cold sweat prickled through his skin.

Jacobs sat down and deJomb walked toward the stage. He had a pleasant, friendly smile on his face.

It dawned on Pete that they must have actually *liked* him. *That's* why they were talking so long. His heart raced. Jupiter was right—Pete was going to be a star. First the Garber, then Broadway . . . did they give a Tony Award for best dancer? Maybe they'd make a category especially for him . . .

DeJomb nodded politely and said the two words that sent Pete crashing back to reality.

"Thank you."

12

Getting into the Act

"**I** KNOW IT WAS MY JUMPING-REVERSE-TURNING KICK," Pete said, pounding his fist into his other palm. "I started off-balance and looked like a total fool." He began pacing the floor of his parents' living room.

Jupiter realized he had created a monster. Pete was so hung up about his audition, he had forgotten about the case. At this rate they'd never find out who was trying to kill George Brandon.

Kelly tousled Pete's hair. "Hey, big guy, you were great. Don't count yourself out yet."

"But they told me 'Thank you'! Jupe said—"

Jupiter cut him off. "Wait a second. They said 'Thank you' to every single person—even though it was the final cut. It's possible they didn't make a decision on the spot. Maybe you're still in the running— maybe I am, too, for that matter. But don't forget, we have to keep our minds on—"

The loud jangling of the phone interrupted him. Pete lurched for the receiver, knocking the phone off its table. It crashed to the floor.

"Hello?" Pete's voice was a high-pitched squeak. Jupiter somehow kept himself from laughing. "Yes . . . I did? You mean me, Pete Crenshaw?"

Jupiter and Kelly rushed to his side. He looked at them with a grin that threatened to crack his cheeks open and mouthed the words "I made it."

Kelly jumped up and down and hugged him. Jupiter clapped his friend on the back. He fought off the voice inside him that said *he* should have been cast too.

As if he read Jupiter's mind, Pete then said into the phone. "Excuse me, Mr. deJomb, what about my friend Jupiter Jones? . . . Yes, I know he's not home— he's here. . . . Sure!" Pete held out the receiver to Jupiter. "He wants to talk to you."

Jupiter tried to control the flutters he felt from head to toe. "Jupiter Jones here."

"Hello, there," came deJomb's voice. "How does it feel to be a featured member of *Danger Zone*?"

"F-featured m-member?" Jupiter could barely get the words out of his mouth. "Why, why, the honor of yours is mine . . . I mean, the honor is . . . what I mean to say is, *yes!*"

DeJomb laughed. "I haven't even told you what the part is."

Jupiter's confidence was soaring. He imagined what he might be playing: George's rival for the heroine, perhaps, or a psychologically complex villain. "I'm rather sure I can handle it, Mr. deJomb," he said with a chuckle. "In addition to my dance training, I've read widely on the Stanislavski Method. I like to think I *inhabit* my characters."

"I'm glad to hear it. You'll be in the scene where George and Anne escape from the cavern and end up on the deserted Japanese beach."

"Yes, I'm familiar with the scene," Jupiter said eagerly.

"Well, we're inserting a new musical number. George has a dream that they're home, at a beach in California. The objects on the beach come to life and start singing and dancing—umbrellas, surfboards, lifeguard chairs, a beachball that gets kicked around . . ."

"A *very* clever idea," Jupiter said.

"And you play the beachball."

Jupiter fell silent.

Kelly and Pete looked at him with concern. "What gives?" Pete whispered.

"I play a *beachball*?" Jupiter finally repeated.

"Yes, you're perfect for the part!" deJomb answered. "A natural comedian! Your audition was so *funny*!"

"It wasn't meant to be funny," Jupiter mumbled.

"Pardon me? Is this a bad connection?"

"No, no. Thank you, I accept, and I look forward to rehearsal."

"Fine. Be over here by three o'clock."

Jupiter hung up.

"Just remember," Pete said with a sympathetic look, "it's all for the case. . . ."

◆   ◆   ◆

Flinging open the door to George's dressing room, Jupiter said, "George—good news!" Pete and Kelly filed in behind him.

They were greeted by the smiling faces of George and Jim Bernardi. "Don't tell me," George said, closing his eyes and putting his hand to his forehead. "You tracked down the ghost of Shakespeare and chained him to a word processor." He smiled. "Just kidding. I heard the news. Congratulations to you both. Jupe, you'll make a great beachball."

"Welcome to the cast," Bernardi said, shaking Jupiter's and Pete's hands. "Now you'll be officially eligible to have some after-rehearsal popcorn." He grabbed a medium-size paper bag that had been sitting on a chair behind him. "Fresh supply."

Jupiter's mouth began to water. But before he could answer, Kelly said, "What a beautiful costume! Is it new?" She walked toward George's costume rack across the room. On it hung a silken robe crisscrossed with many shiny multicolored bands.

A sudden crash made her spin around. A small makeup mirror lay shattered on the floor by George's feet.

"Hey, great coordination, huh?" George exclaimed. "I turned to look at you and knocked my favorite mirror on the floor."

Pete began picking up the pieces. "Broken mirror—bad luck!" he said.

"You sound like Lovell," George commented.

As Jupiter and Kelly joined the cleanup, Bernardi went to the door. "I'm going to call places for the beginning of the new number," he said. "And don't forget to listen for your cues, Jupiter and Pete. I'm told you're *in* this rehearsal."

"Okay, we'll finish this cleanup in no time," George replied.

As soon as they did, they all left the dressing room. Jupiter gave a longing glance at the unopened bag of popcorn. George went over to stage right, from where he would eventually have to make his entrance. Kelly sat down in the audience, while Jupiter and Pete stayed at stage left for their entrances. As they waited, they watched a young man go into George's dressing room carrying scissors and thread. Around his neck was a long measuring tape made of yellow cloth.

"That must be George's dresser," Jupiter said.

"Dresser?" Pete said.

"That's the person in charge of taking care of costumes—hanging them up, making sure they're repaired. We get a dresser, too."

"No kidding? You know, this is *better* than sports. We have to put away our own uniforms."

Jupiter's eye caught a headline in a newspaper lying on a stool nearby.

TEEN IDOL TAKES HIS LUMPS
Shakespeare's Revenge?

He picked it up. Below the headline was a photo of George pointing to the red welt on his forehead where the bust had fallen on him. Underneath, the caption read: "Hard-luck 'Danger Zone' star George Brandon after accident earlier this week."

Pete looked at the photo. "Wow. That picture makes that bump look a lot worse than it really was."

"That's right," Jupiter said, his eyes narrowing. "The next day it was nearly invisible. I bet they developed the picture that way on purpose." He flipped through the paper quickly, arriving at the show-biz gossip page.

"Hey, check this out," Pete said, looking over Jupiter's shoulder. "It says here that Matt Grant just signed a foreign-film deal. I guess Manny Firestone is going to be stuck with George, like it or not!"

"YEEEAAAAGH!" A desperate cry rang out from George's dressing room. Jupiter and Pete dropped the newspaper and raced over, followed by an army of backstage people.

Inside, George's dresser was furiously scratching his right arm, which had turned an angry shade of red.

"What happened?" Jupiter demanded.

The dresser suddenly dove for the sink in the corner

and ran cold water full blast over both arms. "My hands, my arm—they're on fire!"

"Someone call a doctor!" Jupiter shouted over his shoulder. He turned back to the dresser. "How did this happen?"

The dresser's fingernails were now gouging red lines up and down his forearm. "I—I don't know. All I did was touch *that*!"

With a shaking, inflamed finger he pointed to George's brand-new costume.

13

Rash Acts

"*H*ALF-HOUR, PLEASE!" JIM BERNARDI'S VOICE CRACK-led over the backstage speakers. "*Half-hour!*"

"All right, I've got to go," George said into the phone. "I have half an hour to get ready. Thank you for your help. Bye." He turned to Jupiter and Pete. "The doctor was able to tell what kind of skin irritant the cloth was treated with. She gave David an antidote, and he's doing fine."

"Good," Jupiter said. He'd been worried about the dresser all through the afternoon's rehearsal and dinner. "But what about your costume?"

George's eyes were downcast. He answered without his usual energy. "They're giving me another one to use tonight, and they promised to make sure it hasn't been tampered with."

"Are you feeling up to going on tonight?" Pete asked.

"I guess," George said with a shrug. "But I'm getting more and more depressed. On the one hand, I feel terrible for David. But then again, what if *I'd* put that costume on?"

"You'd miss the performance for sure," Jupiter said. "And that's what somebody wants. Now, help us figure out exactly who could have handled your costume today."

George sat back and thought about it. "Well, I think we can count out David—"

"Maybe not. He *could* have messed up the costume and then touched it by mistake," Pete suggested.

"It could have been anyone in the wardrobe department downstairs," George said, "or the costume designer."

Jupiter shook his head. "It seems to me the costume could only have been tampered with *after* it was hung in your room. Otherwise, whoever brought it up would be itching. Unless of course, the irritant was put on a very small area."

"A lot of people have been in my dressing room since the costume was brought up," George said. "Jim Bernaidi, Ron deJomb, Vic Hammil, a few of the actors. It could have been anybody."

The name Vic Hammil leaped out at Jupe. Vic, George's understudy. The hottest suspect for the sticky-fingered basher at Lovell Madeira's apartment. Was Vic trying to create his own lucky breaks?

Jim Bernardi's head suddenly appeared in the doorway. "If you want to see the show, Jupe and Pete, you better get into the house. We're completely sold out, so the ushers are going to have to find a place to put you."

Jupiter and Pete ran out of the dressing room and through the door to the audience. At the back an usher pointed them to a secluded spot near the bar, where Kelly was already standing. There Jupiter could see out to the box office. A line of patient ticket buyers extended into the street.

"It looks as if the show is doing great business," Jupiter said to the usher. His adrenaline pumped as he imagined what it would be like to face a full house from the stage.

"Sold out for three months," the usher replied. "And we're still in previews. Just this past week orders have been flooding in. Who'd have expected it? Before this, we were dead."

As he walked away, Kelly said, "I've been listening to people as they walk in. Everybody's talking about George's accidents. They don't care about the show— it's almost as if they're waiting to see what happens tonight."

"I guess *any* publicity is good for the show," Pete said.

"It's sick, if you ask me," Kelly replied. "What are they going to do—cheer if he gets hurt?"

The lights began to dim and the audience quieted down. As the orchestra started playing the overture, Jupiter noticed that Kelly and Pete were holding hands. Pride was written all over her face, excitement and fear over his.

Jupiter was feeling all those things himself. It wouldn't be long before he and Pete would be hearing that overture from the other side of the curtain. It was a feeling that was making Jupiter drunk with happiness.

And making him slowly forget that there was a mystery to solve.

◆   ◆   ◆

Jupiter, Pete, and Kelly rushed backstage at intermission. George was on the set, walking around and staring at the floor.

"Great job, George!" Kelly called out.

He looked up and smiled. "Thanks. Did you notice where I completely blew the blocking?"

"Blocking?" Pete repeated.

"That's the plan of movement on the stage—exactly where to go, and when."

Something began moving above them. Jupiter jerked his head up.

"Look out!" he shouted, grabbing George and twisting the two of them out of the way.

A wooden door fell from the fly area, narrowly missing George. It stopped, suspended by two heavy ropes, just before reaching the floor.

Jim Bernardi rushed onto the stage. "Johansen!" he bellowed, his eyes narrow with rage.

Bruno peeked out from behind a stage-right curtain. "I don't know what happened, man."

"Whaddaya mean, you don't know what happened?" Bernardi demanded.

"Hey, look, *you* were the one who told me to run that cue. Cool your jets."

A hush fell across the stage. Bernardi looked as if he would explode. He walked menacingly toward Bruno. "What—do—you—mean, 'cool my jets'?" he hissed. "You're supposed to check the stage, too, you lummox. You know I have blind spots from where I stand. I'm fed up with all these so-called accidents!"

"Oh, are you framing *me* now?" Bruno turned toward Bernardi, clenching and unclenching his fists. "Whose lousy cues have caused all the other accidents, huh? Who yells at *you* when you screw up, you senile old has-been? This show would be a lot better off without you."

Bernardi charged him, his fists drawn. Immediately four burly stagehands held him back. "Easy, Jim," one of them said. "You know how he gets."

"Better off without me, huh?" Bernardi said, seething. "Well, maybe I'll show you how this place falls apart without me." He spun around and headed for the exit. "*He's* the one behind all this. He's just covering his tail!"

"Liar," Bruno shot back.

But the only answer from Bernardi was the sharp slamming of the stage door.

Jupiter, Pete, Kelly, and a group of stagehands ran after him. They crowded into the hallway behind Luther, who had left his office to see what had happened.

A few people ran outside, others urged that Bernardi

be left alone. Eventually everyone filtered back inside, leaving the second act to be run by the assistant stage manager.

Luther checked the pegboard on his door. "Terrific. He forgot to return his office key." Muttering, he trundled inside.

Jupiter walked back into the wings. "No, he didn't," he whispered to Pete and Kelly.

"Didn't what?" Pete asked.

"Forget to return his key." With a sly grin, Jupiter pulled a small key chain out of his pocket. "I took it off the pegboard in the confusion. We have to search Bernardi's office—to find out if he's behind all the accidents or not. If he isn't the one, I'm sure we can dig up useful information about the rest of the crew."

Pete smiled. "Right on, Beachball!"

◆   ◆   ◆

The amber light from Pete's flashlight circled the office. It was well after midnight, and they had seen no one in the theater when they had broken in.

"Did you hear that?" Pete suddenly whispered.

"Yes, I think it was your heart beating," Jupiter answered. "Now, would you mind giving me some light?"

Pete trained the flashlight on a folder Jupiter had in his hand. PERSONNEL was written across the front.

"Let's see . . . John Everson, Scott Harris . . . Here we are. Bruno Johansen."

"What's it say?" Pete whispered, looking around nervously.

"A note about one arrest for a bar brawl. That's it."
He snapped the folder shut. "This appears to be fruit-
less. None of Bernardi's own records show anything,
and the only person with anything suspicious on file is
Luther, who's on parole for a felony conviction."

"Okay, let's make tracks."

"Yeah, let's go." Jupiter put the folder back in a file
cabinet and opened the door. He stumbled on the way
out and caught himself against the doorjamb with his
left arm.

They crept through the basement area. Pete's flashlight brought them to the stairs that led up to the stage.
As Jupiter grabbed the banister, he felt a shooting pain
in his left arm. "Yeow!" he said, stopping to scratch it.

"What's the matter?" came Pete's panicked voice.

"Nothing, just an itch." He climbed a couple of
steps, but the itch intensified. He stopped again. He
dug his fingernails into his skin to relieve the pain. "A
horrible itch!"

"Jupe," Pete said, "this is unbelievably weird."

Jupiter knew exactly what his friend meant. This
had to be the same itch George's dresser had suffered.
Jupe thought back to their encounter with Bernardi in
the dressing room just before the dresser touched the
sabotaged costume. "I have a feeling that bag of popcorn Bernardi had—"

Pete finished the sentence: "—wasn't really a bag of
popcorn."

"Are *you* itching?" Jupiter asked, continuing to the
top of the stairs.

"No."

"It must have been the doorjamb. Bernardi probably spilled some on it, or rubbed a glove against it that had touched the—"

A quick series of dull thumping noises made him stop.

"*That* wasn't my heart," Pete whispered.

Jupiter's eyes strained to pick out the shadows backstage. "It came from downstage left. Come on!"

They raced to the source of the noise—Bernardi's computer station in the wing. But the only trace of a human being was the glow of the computer monitor. Pete shone his flashlight all around.

"Cut the light," a gruff voice called out from behind them, "or you'll be sorry!"

Jupiter's heart leaped. "Do what he says," he urged his friend.

Pete obeyed. They both turned slowly around toward the black curtain in back of them.

Aimed right at them, shining dully in the light of the monitor screen, was the barrel of a pistol.

14

Phantom of
the Operating System

"RAISE YOUR HANDS, TURN AROUND, AND WALK straight," the voice said.

Jupiter and Pete stepped slowly forward. In front of them was George's dressing room. Its door was slightly ajar.

"Go through that door and stand against the wall at the other end," the voice continued.

Jupiter pushed the door open with his foot. A small, neon-lit clock near George's mirror cast a purplish glow in the room. Jupiter and Pete headed for the wall, carefully avoiding the clothes rack. Jupiter's arm still itched like crazy.

There was a click, and the room's lights went on. Jupiter flinched at the sudden brightness.

"Well, will you look who the cat dragged in," the voice said.

Jupiter turned around. A .38-caliber revolver stared him in the face. It was held steady by a pair of taut, outstretched arms—arms that extended from the broad shoulders of Luther Sharpe.

"I thought the voice was familiar," Jupiter said. He resumed scratching his arm.

Luther glared at him. "So *you're* the ones!" he said.

Pete and Jupiter exchanged blank looks. "We're *what* ones?" Pete asked.

They jumped back as Luther tightened his grip. "Don't mess with me. You guys are in hot water. I saw you fooling with that computer."

"Hey, wait a minute. That wasn't us!" Pete protested.

"Tell it to the police, pal," Luther said. He took one hand off the gun and reached for the phone.

"That'll be easy enough," Jupiter said with a nonchalant shrug. "But *you* better figure out what to say to your parole officer when we tell him you have a gun." He let the words sink in as he lowered his arms. Then he walked over to the sink in the corner of the room. "Now, if you'll excuse me . . ."

Luther's hand rested on the telephone. He narrowed his eyes at Jupiter. "My parole officer . . . how did you find out about him?"

"My guess is he doesn't know about the gun." As Jupiter let a steady gush of cold tap water run over his left arm, soothing his itch, he smiled at Luther.

"All right, you win." Luther lowered the gun. "But you two better scram, you hear me?"

"Not so fast," Pete said. "What were *you* doing around that computer at this time of night?"

"I *work* here, kid, in case you didn't notice. Six days a week, plus graveyard shift on Thursdays. I was sitting over on stage right and I guess I dozed off. When I woke up, I saw the shadow of somebody messing with the computer."

"What kind of shadow?" Jupiter pressed. "What did the person look like?"

Luther frowned as he examined Pete. "Come to think of it, he was kind of short—not at all like you. He was skinny, too." He looked at Jupiter. "*Definitely* not like you."

Jupiter decided to let that one pass. But instinctively he sucked in his stomach.

"Look," Luther said, folding his arms, "you got my number. I can't tell anyone about you, because you'll mess up my parole. But if you guys know anything, you know I *care* about this job and this theater. So you can at least tell me what you're doing here. I got a feeling you're more than pals of George."

Pete shot Jupiter an uncertain look.

Jupiter thought about it a moment, then nodded. "Mr. Sharpe, this has to remain a secret. I must have your promise—"

Luther's eyes lit up. "*You* guys must be the detectives, right?"

Jupiter's jaw dropped. He stopped rubbing his arm.

"Who told you?" Pete demanded.

"Nobody had to tell me," Luther replied, excited. "It's in the papers!"

"That *can't* be!" Jupiter said.

"Sure!" Luther took a folded-up tabloid out of his

rear pants pocket and flipped through it. "It says right here: 'Two private undercover detectives have been hired to investigate the mysterious happenings, a confidential source said.' " He looked up. "Heck, we was all wondering who the detectives could be—or even if there really *was* any! No one ever thought it would be *cast members*."

"Well, I congratulate you on your discovery," Jupiter said, trying to keep cool, "but it's *really* important not to tell *any*one."

"Hey, you can count on Luther, my friends. I'm *glad* you guys are here."

"Thank you," Jupiter replied. "Now, if you don't mind . . ."

Drying his arm against his jeans, Jupiter walked out of the dressing room and headed for the computer. Pete followed and Luther went back to his office. The screen showed a list of cues, above which were the words EDIT MODE.

"Looks Greek to me," Pete said

"Possibly a Greek *tragedy*, if we don't figure out what was tampered with," Jupiter replied.

"Maybe a tragedy by Shakespeare," Pete said darkly.

"Cut the superstition, Pete. What we need is hard evidence," Jupiter said.

"Look at all those crazy numbers and codes," Pete said. "How're you going to figure them out?"

"That may not be necessary." Jupiter scanned the

list of function keys at the bottom of the screen. "Here we go. F8—'repeat last function.' That ought to tell us something."

It did. When Jupiter hit it, one cue immediately erased itself. They watched as the screen scrolled up a few times. Another cue disappeared, and the first cue popped into its spot. Then the screen scrolled back down.

"Hey, it exchanged two cues!" Pete said. "Maybe it's setting up the next accident!"

"Or erasing the last one. Don't forget, we're watching a command that was just given. Maybe someone was deleting errors that he had introduced before."

"Just to be on the safe side, I'll quit without saving, so it'll return to where it was before anyone touched it tonight," Jupiter said, placing his fingers over the keyboard.

Then he carefully quit the program. Jupiter and Pete said good-bye to Luther and left the theater. Their footsteps echoed down the cool, empty street as they walked to Jupiter's pickup, which they'd parked several blocks away to avoid suspicion.

Jupiter's left arm felt fine again. The water had done the trick. Jupiter realized he must have only gotten a small dosage of the irritant.

"How the heck did the papers find out about us?" Pete wondered. "We swore George to secrecy!"

Jupiter shrugged. "Perhaps George let it slip."

"He would have told us."

"Unless he didn't want to tell us. Maybe he's involved. After all, he has a run-of-the-play contract. Even if he's put out of commission, he can sit at home and collect a paycheck."

Pete thought about that. "I guess. But George seems like the kind of guy who wants to be where the action is—not sitting on his duff."

"The big question is, who's sabotaging the computer?"

"It's *got* to be Bernardi," Pete said. "He's the one calling the cues."

"Yes, but why would he sneak into the theater late at night to change them? He could do it himself during the day—no one would question him. Besides, he said he doesn't know how to do the programming."

"Uh-huh. And he's definitely not short and skinny."

Jupiter exhaled. "Who do we know who's short and skinny and knows something about computer programming?"

Pete looked at him blankly

"Okay, what kinds of people would know programming?" Jupe asked. "Systems analysts, some writers . . ."

"Students, musicians . . ."

Jupiter stopped short. "Musicians?"

"Yeah. You know how Bob's always talking about those guys who program drum tracks and can make synthesizers sound like any instrument they want."

"I *do* know. And I remember talking about one of

those guys in particular. One who was very near a certain flash-pot explosion, yet miraculously managed to escape without a scorch."

Pete's face lit up. "Well, I'll be a . . ."

"Pete, I think Shakespeare's ghost is none other than Buzz Newman."

15

A Star Is Born

THE EARLY MORNING SUN GLARED THROUGH THE PICK-
up's windshield as Jupiter drove into the Garber
Theater parking lot.

"I can't believe they can just *do* this!" Pete said,
sipping a cup of coffee. "I mean, how can they make
us go on today? Is it normal to hire people on a Thursday and make them perform on Sunday?"

Jupiter yawned. "I don't think they have any choice,
Pete. They have to put the new musical numbers into
the show quickly. We open next week. That's why
we've been rehearsing twelve hours a day."

Pete railroaded on. "And the worst part is that they
woke us up to tell us!"

Jupiter parked, then got out of the pickup. "Hey,
come on, it was just a reminder call. They figured we
were up already. I mean, we've been getting up this
early anyway to rehearse for the last two days."

"Yeah, but I was counting on sleeping—"

"Till the very last minute! Just remember, you were
sleeping while *I* was up calling Bob."

"I'm sure you made his day. I bet he didn't roll in till the wee hours."

Jupiter nodded. "You've got it, but he wasn't out with one of his harem. He got in at three in the morning from a two-day road trip to San Francisco. But when I told him our new suspicions about Buzz, he was all ears. He said he'd hang out with Buzz today after rehearsal and try to pick something up."

They walked through the stage door and onto the stage. Behind the black curtain that hid Jim Bernardi's station came the steady clicking of a computer keyboard.

"Hey, Jimbo!" Pete called out. "We're here! A little early, but ready to go!"

The clicking stopped. No one answered.

"Jim?" Jupiter said. He moved closer to the station and pulled the curtain aside.

George Brandon turned from the monitor with his finger to his mouth. "Shhh," he said. "He'll kill me if he knows I'm here."

Jupiter lowered his voice. "What are you doing?"

George indicated a large loose-leaf book that was lying open on the computer stand. "This is a hard copy of the cues. Jim keeps it on a shelf under the computer. He made it weeks ago and has been updating it by hand as changes are made." He looked left and right. "I was comparing it to the computer to see if there's been any tampering. To tell you the truth, I'm not so sure Jim's innocent."

"No kidding," Pete said, his voice showing a trace of anger. "So why are *you*—"

"Easy, Pete," Jupiter said. He could understand Pete's frustration. George had hired *them* to do the investigating. "Uh, I believe this matter is a bit more delicate than you realize, George. You see, if you're trying to solve this case on your own, you're sabotaging what *we're* doing. For instance, you could have told us about this book."

George nodded. "I *tried* to. The minute I thought of it last night, I called and left a message on your answering machine. Didn't you get it?"

Jupiter shook his head and sighed. The HQ machine must have been acting up again.

"Anyway, I figured I'd get here bright and early, before Jim did, and then I'd tell you about it later." He smiled. "Hey, I know you guys are the pros. I was just trying to help."

"Did you find anything?" Jupiter asked.

George hesitated. "Uh, no. Not yct. But I'll keep looking."

Jupiter wasn't completely convinced. George seemed a little defensive and nervous, and something about his story didn't hold up. Was he keeping information from them—and if so, why?

At the sudden sound of voices in the corridor, George quickly turned off the computer and put the book back.

"Hey, is everybody here already?" came Bernardi's voice.

He entered, followed by Ron deJomb, Craig Jacobs, and three of the other cast members.

"Almost," Jupiter replied, counting everyone. "We're missing two."

"Okay, then why don't we run Pete in the Japanese screen number," Bernardi said. "We've got to turn you into a star by tonight!"

Pete and Jupe exchanged glances. It was going to be a long day.

◆   ◆   ◆

Pete rehearsed with an energy he never knew he had. Despite warnings from deJomb to take it easy, Pete attacked each dance move with furious intensity. His kicks soared, his punches snapped.

After his dance was over, he tried to stay calm. He talked very little through the rest of the rehearsal and the start of the evening performance. But something began happening inside of him at the start of the second act.

He should have been laughing. From his vantage point in the wings he had a great view of the beach scene. Jupiter leaped around the stage in an overblown multicolored beachball getup, keeping a straight face.

Smash! Jupe flattened George against another actor dressed as a giant trash can. *Whop!* George rolled Jupe back against a human beach umbrella. Jupe's face was red with heat and embarrassment. But the audience loved the number. They roared their approval.

Looking on, Pete felt nothing but a black, over-whelming dread. He found himself hoping the num-

ber would never end. When it did, a smiling,
triumphant Jupiter bounded offstage.

Pete slapped Jupe on the back halfheartedly. They
stood together silently until the first chords of "Kyoto
con Moto" floated through the curtain and into the
wings.

Pete froze.

"I can't, Jupe, I *can't!*" he whispered. His heart
pounded so hard that his shirt moved to the beat. He
couldn't get the cold sweat off his hands, he couldn't
stop his knees from shaking. "I think something's
wrong with me."

Jupiter smiled. His polyester beachball costume
bunched up as he tried to put an arm around Pete.
"It's an age-old malady known as stage fright. I promise you it will go away the second you walk in front of
the audience."

"*Audience?*" The word hit Pete with the impact of
a cattle prod. "There are *people* out there! Bob and
Kelly too. They all paid lots of money. What if they all
walk out when I come onstage? What if they demand
their money back?"

"Listen," Jupiter said grimly. "If they didn't walk
out when they saw me humiliating myself as a piece of
recreational equipment, they're here for the duration.
Trust me."

In spite of himself, Pete smiled.

"At least I got your mind off the fact that it's time for
your entrance."

"My—" Pete swallowed. There it was, the lilting Japanese harmony that began his dance. The lights had brightened. The other dancers were already moving behind the screen. A voice crept into the back of his mind, a voice that seemed to crackle over a loudspeaker: *"It's fourth and goal for the Rocky Beach Warriors. They decline the field goal. Crenshaw enters the game!"*

The next sound was an explosive roar from the stands. Pete could see thousands of football fans rising to their feet, screaming his name. His blood began to flow again, his stomach to settle, his eyes to focus. The dancers had started moving away from center stage.

Pete was ready. He took a deep breath, and with a bloodcurdling *kiai* shout that welled up from deep within, he leaped onto the stage.

The next few minutes passed in a blur. He was aware of his fists and legs thrusting. He saw the stage floor receding and then speeding closer to him as he leaped. He felt his body in sync with the music. His one lingering fear—that the turntable would move during his leap—never came about.

Then it was over. Just like that. Pete wasn't even sure he heard the applause. He vaguely recalled Bernardi saying "Noice job."

The rest of the play passed by in a fog. But when it was over, Pete was *definitely* aware of the standing ovation that greeted his curtain call.

◆   ◆   ◆

"WHOOO-AAAAH!" Pete clutched Kelly to his side as he shouted out the window of the pickup.

"Shhh," Kelly said, dissolving into giggles. Outside

the theater, startled patrons watched the pickup leave the parking lot.

Jupiter laughed. "They think you're a star, Pete. Keep up the image."

"I don't care!" Pete shouted. "I want to *party!* Let's have some rock!"

He flicked on the radio—a classical music station . . . a baseball game . . . news . . .

He groaned at the choices. "If Andrews was here, he'd have some good tapes. Why did he have to stay late with those musicians?"

"He'll catch up with us," Jupiter said. "Hey, turn back to that last station!"

"Aw, come on, Jupe," Pete complained. "You can hear the news later!"

"That was George's voice!" Jupiter replied. "It must be a taped interview."

Pete found the station. A silken-voiced announcer was saying, "I understand, George, that despite all the mishaps, there has been a turnaround in the show's fortunes. In fact, *Variety* reports that *Danger Zone* has the biggest advance sale of any show in the history of the Garber Theater."

"That's right, Dan," George's enthusiastic voice answered. "You know, a few days ago I was worried about losing this job—not to mention my life!"

"Amazing, the turns life takes," the announcer said. "There was talk of your role going to Matt Grant, and now it looks like you'll be going on to Broadway and much, much bigger things."

"Well," George replied, "I guess old William Shakespeare must have given up the ghost!"

"George sounds as if the death threats have vanished into thin air," said Jupe.

Suddenly it all became clear. Jupiter slammed on the brakes. "I've got it!" he shouted.

The screech of another car's brakes made them all spin around.

"What's that turkey doing?" Pete said. "He can pass us."

But Jupiter knew. "We're being followed. Hang on, guys, for a ride to remember."

16

Follow the Leader

JUPITER JAMMED THE GAS PEDAL DOWN. THE PICKUP flew around the nearest corner, clipping the curb.

Pete's head smacked against the roof. "Yeow! What are you doing? I have a *public* to face tomorrow!"

"This is no joke, Pete!" Jupiter yelled. He shot a glance into his rearview mirror. The sports car behind them careened around the corner.

Kelly looked out the back window. "J-Jupiter's right," she said, her eyes wide with fright.

"Maybe they want my autograph," Pete said. But the humor in his voice had faded.

Jupiter yanked the steering wheel to the left. The right side of the pickup rose off the ground. Kelly screamed.

"Where are you going, Jupe?" Pete cried.

"I don't know!" The pickup jounced over a pothole. Pete clutched the top of his head—an instant too late.

"Get off the streets! That car is faster than yours!"

The crack of a gunshot rang out. "Duck!" Pete shouted, pushing Kelly to the floor.

Jupiter swerved. He wasn't going to make it. No way. The sports car was gaining. On his left the block stretched out for what looked like miles, lined by the tall trees of a country club. On the right the block was broken only by the entrance to an enormous building, an indoor shopping mall. Unlit neon letters reading PARK hung over the entrance, which was blocked by a striped barricade.

Turning sharply, Jupiter headed into the barricade. A yellow CLOSED sign rushed toward them.

"Jupe, what are you doing?" Kelly screamed from the floor. She buried her face in her arms.

There was a jolt and a crash of splintering wood. Jupiter accelerated into the parking garage. His head pushed backward against the seat as the pickup climbed a ramp.

"There's a good bookstore on the fourth floor," Jupiter remarked.

"You've *got* to be kidding!" Pete yelled.

Kelly grabbed the dashboard and peered out the windshield. "We'll be trapped, Jupiter!"

"Not if we lose them on one of the levels," Jupiter answered. They were spiraling upward . . . upward . . .

The sixth floor was the roof. They shot out of the ramp and onto a wide expanse of asphalt, neatly marked with parallel white lines and completely empty. Against the wall to their left, a tiny glass elevator entrance jutted above a narrow sidewalk. Next to the elevator was a stairwell.

The pickup's engine was the only noise Jupiter heard as they roared across the lot. Were they alone? He looked into the rearview mirror again. The ramp exit was a black hole now at least fifty yards behind them.

"I think we lost them," he said.

"Great," Pete remarked. "What now? We drive off the roof and land on the freeway?"

Jupiter scanned the four corners of the roof. Diagonally across from them was the exit ramp. He gunned the accelerator and headed straight for it.

Until the exit began to glow with an increasingly intense light.

"It's them!" Kelly shrieked.

Jupiter hit the brake. The tires let out a high-pitched scream.

Pete started to yell a warning. "Step on the—"

With a cough and a sputter the pickup stalled.

"—clutch."

"Thanks, Pete," Jupiter said. He turned the ignition key and ground the starter.

Like a serpent's eyes, two headlights appeared in the ramp exit.

Rrrrrr . . . ca-chunk. The engine was dead. Jupiter tried again.

Rrrrrr . . . ca-chunk.

"Let's get out of here!" Pete cried. He grabbed Kelly by the arm and flung open the door.

The three of them raced toward the stairwell. Their

shadows stretched before them, tapering from giant legs to grotesquely narrow heads in the backlight of the sports car's high beams.

But they were gaining ground. Another twenty feet . . .

The high beams veered abruptly to the right. Then in a flash of slick, black metal, the car swerved in front of them. It jerked upward as it climbed the pavement, blocking the entrance to the stairwell.

"I've got a gun, and I'll use it!" a gruff voice shouted. Both doors swung open.

The first thing Jupiter saw was the glint of a pistol. He put his arms in the air and was relieved when his friends did the same.

They were soon face to face with two men wearing dark ski masks. The driver carried the gun. "Who are you?" Pete demanded.

"Move!" was the only answer he got. The driver waved his gun toward the brick wall that surrounded the rooftop.

Jupiter's stomach sank. "You're not going to make us—"

"Move!" the driver repeated. Over his shoulder he barked a command to his accomplice. "Don't just stand there! Take care of the pickup."

Despite the panic that raced through Jupiter's brain, he could tell that the driver was disguising his voice. It had an unnatural, guttural quality.

The other man hesitated, then reached into the

sports car. He pulled out a full liquor bottle and two large pocket flasks and started walking toward Jupiter's pickup.

"Wh-what are you doing?" Jupiter sputtered. "That's my uncle's truck!"

The gunman let out a low chuckle. "Perfect. I can hear it now: 'Three teens—star dancer, girlfriend, and beachball sidekick—go for drunken joyride in borrowed car and stumble off rooftop to death. News at eleven.' "

"Drunken . . . we never . . ." Jupiter heard splashing noises. He looked over to see the other man emptying the pocket flasks onto the seat of Uncle Titus's pickup. "Hey, he can't—"

"You're right, he can't," the gunman said. He shouted to his accomplice, "Hey! Save some for the kids! We need enough to get their blood-alcohol levels up!"

The other man tossed the pocket flasks into the pickup and approached with the bottle.

Pete's eyes bulged with rage. "You rotten—!" He reared back with his fists.

"Pete! Don't!" Jupiter shouted.

The man holding the gun pointed it at Pete's face. "Listen to your friend."

Pete backed off, seething.

"At least this way," the gunman continued, grabbing the bottle from his accomplice, "you'll feel much less pain." Glaring at Pete, he unscrewed the bottle and thrust it at him. "Okay, Bruce Lee, *open wide!*"

"Pete . . ." Kelly's voice was somewhere between a moan, a warning, and a prayer.

Pete trembled as the bottle came close to his lips. His teeth were clenched, but his eyes betrayed indecision as they stared into the barrel of the gun. Slowly he parted his lips.

The sudden sound of an engine made the gunman spin around. "What the—"

Without missing a beat, Kelly lowered her shoulders and charged the gunman. She connected with a square hit just above the belt.

The gunman managed a strangled cry of surprise as he stumbled backward. His pistol flew into the air.

As it clattered to the blacktop, Pete dove on top of it like a defensive lineman recovering a fumble.

"Leave it, Pete!" Jupiter called out.

Pete looked up to see both men scrambling into the sports car. Jupiter and Kelly both clung to the doors, but they had to let go as the car began to speed away.

Out of the exit ramp emerged the source of the engine sound—a red Volkswagen bug.

"It's Bob!" Jupiter shouted in amazement.

The sports car took off toward the entrance. Putt-putting feebly, the Volkswagen chased after it.

In seconds Jupiter, Pete, and Kelly were in the pickup. This time it started instantly, and they sped past the Volkswagen and onto the descending ramp.

"It said 'no exit' above the opening," Kelly said. "Does that mean—"

"That's the least of our worries!" Pete shouted.

Jupiter's face puckered at the sickly sweet odor of alcohol. Uncle Titus was going to have a fit when he smelled his truck. Jupe tried to ignore it, guiding the pickup downward. It careened off the rubber guards on the sharply curved walls.

At the bottom the walls became foot-high curbs as the ramp leveled into a long straightaway. A good thirty yards ahead of them, the sports car roared toward a large red sign that said ENTRANCE ONLY. Beyond the sign was the street.

"They're going to make it!" Pete slammed the dashboard in frustration.

Jupiter suddenly took his foot off the gas pedal and smiled. "No, they're not."

A hideous squeal filled the ground floor of the garage. The sports car swerved to the left, the right . . .

With a sudden jounce its front end hit the curb and sailed straight upward. The car came down smack on the curb, sending both passengers flying out the doors and onto the ground.

Jupiter put on his brakes. The pickup came to a stop ten feet from the two inert bodies. Next to them the sports car hung over the curb like an unoccupied seesaw.

The entrance was now clearly visible. Across the entire width was a set of sharp metal spikes, pointed straight at them like swords poised for battle. The sports car had stopped just short of them.

"I always hated those things," Pete said. "But not anymore."

Jupiter jumped out of the pickup and ran toward the men. Pete and Kelly followed hard on his heels. Bob pulled up in his VW and joined them.

Jupiter knelt next to the deathly still accomplice and yanked off his mask.

Vic Hammil's face lolled lazily to the left.

Beside him, Bob pulled off the gunman's mask.

Jim Bernardi.

17

All Played Out

KELLY STARED AT THE TWO BODIES IN HORROR. "ARE they—dead?"

Jupiter felt for both their pulses. "No. But I don't think they'll feel so great when they wake up."

"I'll call an ambulance," Pete said. He ran to a pay phone just inside the entrance.

"This is awful," Kelly said, sitting on the ground. "I was always a little suspicious of Vic, but Jim Bernardi was such a nice guy."

"I have news for you both—they weren't the only ones involved," Bob said. "Looks like you were right, Jupe. I did some snooping around the musicians' lockers and found this in Buzz's." He pulled an envelope out of his jacket and handed it to Jupiter.

Jupiter took out a folded sheet of yellow legal paper covered with numbers and instructions. "These are cues and cue numbers—including the ones that were tampered with the other night."

"So *Buzz* was in on this too," Kelly said. "But why?"

Jupiter folded up the paper and put it into his

pocket. "We haven't gotten to the bottom of this. We have to flush out the ringleader."

Pete rushed over from the pay phone. "An ambulance is on the way," he called out.

"Sounds like you know who this ringleader is," Jupe," Bob said.

"There's one person who benefits the most from spectacular attempts on George's life." Jupiter paused, savoring the looks of anticipation on his friends' faces.

"Who?" Pete demanded.

"Well, let me put it this way. It all started to fit together when I heard that interview on the car radio—the one where George talked about how happy he was about the box-office boom. He mentioned that if it weren't for that, he'd be out of a job."

"Well, we knew *that* already," Kelly said. "At Bud's Healthworks he told us the show's success could mean a move to Broadway, then movie contracts and fame and fortune."

"And fame and fortune have been the most important goals in George Brandon's life," Jupiter said. "It's clear from all the self-congratulatory material he has on his walls, the fact that he uses his own publicist, the ruthlessness with which he argued with Firestone about staying in the show—"

"We all know the guy's an egomaniac," Pete interrupted. "What're you getting at?"

"Before the accidents happened, the show was in danger of closing. Now, within two weeks, it's become a huge hit—and it hasn't even officially opened yet! What caused the change?"

Pete shrugged. "The publicity in all the papers."

"Exactly," Jupiter said. "Publicity. Every time something happened, the papers snapped it right up—even when there was no reporter anywhere near the theater."

Bob finally spoke up. "Which means someone was tipping off publicity agents or the press."

Jupiter nodded. "Someone to whom publicity meant everything. Someone who knew that publicity was the only thing that could keep him from losing his job."

"George," Pete said under his breath.

"Think about it," Jupiter went on. "You're a young actor in a show that's potentially a hit. You can taste the success you've dreamed about your whole life. But something you did causes ticket sales to drop off, and now things look bleak. You're going to be fired, or the show will close—either way, you're back to being just another starving actor. What would you do?"

Pete shrugged. "Become an auto mechanic."

"You'd think of a way to make yourself absolutely necessary for the show's success," Jupiter said. "We all know that most people come to see *Danger Zone* nowadays because of George—or what might happen to him."

"Makes sense," Pete said.

"*I* don't think so!" Kelly said. "How could he have done all those dangerous things to himself?"

"He didn't," Jupiter replied. "We never saw any proof of the bogus phone calls and letters he received. He said he threw the letters away—but I bet he never got any. He had expert help with the accidents, people who would make sure that nothing really bad happened to him. That sign outside the theater—did you notice how far away from George it actually fell?"

"Yes, but right where the TV cameras could pick it up!" Kelly exclaimed.

"And the flash-pot explosion looked dangerous too," Pete said, "but it just *happened* to go off when George was turning away from it."

"Buzz could have controlled the timing from the orchestra pit," Bob suggested.

"Under Bernardi's supervision," Jupiter added. "Anyway, after it happened, we went into George's dressing room and he was on the phone with someone named Ruthie. It didn't mean much to me until I remembered the name of his publicist."

"Ruth Leslie!" Pete exclaimed. "He phoned her to leak the news. And now I know how Luther got the dope on us from the papers. George told the papers about us himself. We were his ticket to more free publicity!"

"Right," said Jupe. "And it looks as if Buzz was taking care of the computer end the whole time, sneaking into the theater, switching numbers for certain cues—with Bernardi's blessing. As stage manager, Bernardi could engineer it all."

"Until we almost caught Buzz in the act," Pete said. "I guess George took over the computer then."

"Or else we just caught George this morning reviewing Buzz's work," Jupiter said. "After all, if he didn't know exactly which cues were which, he'd *really* be in trouble."

"So between that night and this morning, you guys surprised both Buzz *and* George tampering with the show," Bob said. "You were too close to blowing the whole thing open. No wonder they came after you tonight!"

"Wait a minute! What about the itching stuff and the bust of Shakespeare?" Kelly asked.

Pete spoke up. "Remember the day George got his new costume? Bernardi left the dressing room with a bag that he said had popcorn in it—that must have been the poison. He'd probably just finished sabotaging the costume. And remember how you were about to touch it, Kelly, when George dropped his mirror? *That* got our attention."

"George and Vic obviously engineered the accident with Shakespeare's bust," Jupe continued. "They probably thought of it on the way over to Lovell's. Both of them ate the sticky buns, so that's why both the light switch and the bust were sticky. George lowered the bust to the floor while Vic yanked the light cord. Nobody saw them because our eyes were closed!"

"I don't know," Kelly said. "George had a heavy-duty bruise on his forehead."

"But somehow it managed to disappear the next day," Pete said.

"It was probably makeup," Jupe said. "George could have had a red wax stick in his pocket and rubbed some onto his forehead."

"Okay, how about the turntable?" asked Kelly. "Did George really set out to hurt that poor dancer?"

"Nah, it's Bernardi who controls the turntable," said Pete.

Kelly nodded. "Okay, you guys have figured out this whole big plot. But what I don't understand is, *why* did those other guys help George out?"

"Vic was probably worried about his job, just as George was," Jupiter answered. "And I know Buzz was concerned about money. That's all he and Bob talked about when Buzz visited Headquarters. Don't forget, it's incredibly hard to get steady work as an actor or a musician."

"Or as a stage manager, I guess," Pete added.

Jupiter shook his head. "That's what I don't understand. Stage managers tend to work a lot. From what I hear, the good ones go from job to job—and to have been hired for a complex show like *Danger Zone*, Bernardi must be a good one."

Pete's forehead suddenly creased. "You know, the turntable accident doesn't make any sense. If Bernardi thought the dancer was George, why would he have started the turntable? The idea was to keep George in the show."

"But he was the stage manager!" Kelly replied. "He *must* have known it wasn't George."

Bob shook his head. "Then why would he risk injuring a dancer and having to replace him so close to opening?"

They all looked at Jupiter.

"I'm not sure," Jupiter said with a smile. "But I can guess how to find out. Who does this sound like?" In a nasal accent that seemed to come straight from New York, he said, "Let's get adda heah as soon as da fuzz gets heah."

"That's Bernardi," Kelly guessed.

Pete rolled his eyes. "A great time to be doing imitations, Jupe."

"Follow me." Jupiter led them to the pay phone. He picked it up, deposited coins, and punched in George's number. Pete, Kelly, and Bob crowded around him, each with an ear close to the receiver.

"Hello?" came George's breathless voice.

"Yeah," Jupiter answered in his Jim Bernardi accent. "It's Jim."

"Did you get them?" George asked.

"Uh-huh," Jupiter replied.

"Whew. It's a relief, Jim. I mean, I feel terrible about it, but you were right. Jupiter saw me messing with the computer, and he would have blown the whole thing."

"Mm-hmm."

"How about Vic? Did you get him?"

Jupiter's breath caught in his throat. The others stared at him blankly.

"Answer me, Jim! I'm getting an ulcer here!"

"Yeah," was all Jupiter said.

"Talkative, aren't you?" George's voice was dry with sarcasm. "Okay, I'll have your check tomorrow."

The words landed heavily in Jupiter's ear. It was a simple matter of money. Bernardi was being paid off.

Jupiter paused. It didn't make sense to confront George over the phone. He'd wait until tomorrow—in the theater, where the people who mattered could hear it.

Softly Jupiter said, "See ya," and hung up the phone.

He relayed George's end of the conversation to his friends. For what seemed like ages no one said a word.

"Well, I guess we got the last pieces of the puzzle," Bob finally said.

Pete's face was twisted with a frown. "But why was George after Vic?"

"My guess is that Vic rebelled," Jupiter said. "He must have been the one who pulled the turntable stunt. With all the backstage confusion during the new number, he could have passed by and tripped the switch. It's possible he didn't know they'd gotten a dancer to substitute for George in the number."

"But Vic had nothing against George, did he?" Bob asked.

"Not until George's plan got to be so successful," Jupiter replied. "Once it looked like the show was going to be a hit, and Matt Grant was out of the picture, who had the best shot at stardom if George had to leave the show with an injury?"

"His understudy," Pete said.

The distant squeal of a siren broke the silence.

"There's the ambulance," Bob said.

Jupiter nodded and reached for the phone again. "I guess we can call the cops now. I'm sure they'll want to ask our friends some interesting questions at the hospital."

As Jupiter punched 911, Kelly glanced back at their two inert assailants. "Unreal," she said. "They seemed like such okay guys."

"Okay guys whose plan for success got way out of control," Bob remarked.

Jupiter looked knowingly at his friends. "That's show biz!"

18

There's No Business Like . . .

T HE BREEZE THAT BLEW IN THROUGH THE COURTHOUSE
door had an edge of coolness. It was one of those
rare November days when the Los Angeles tempera-
ture goes below sixty. Jupiter zipped up his Wind-
breaker as he walked toward the door with Pete, Bob,
and Kelly.

"That dancer's lawyer really lit into George, didn't
she?" Kelly said. "Sounds like he's going to have to
pay a lot of money for that turntable accident."

"That's nothing compared to what the union's lawyers are going to do to him in their trial," Pete replied.
"And the investors' lawyers in *theirs*."

"I can't say I blame them," Jupiter remarked. "A lot
of people lost a lot of money when the show closed—
not to mention all the actors who were put out of
work."

"I guess once George and Vic were fired, and Bernardi was suspended by the union, and the whole
mystery was solved, people lost interest in the show,"

Pete said. "I couldn't believe how fast the cancellations came pouring in."

"I didn't think the show was that great, anyway," Bob commented.

"But it was my big break," Pete lamented. "And I only got to perform twice!"

"Oh, no," said Jupe. "He's stagestruck!"

They all laughed.

The frantic murmur of crowd noise got louder as they approached the entrance. They walked out into the cloudy afternoon and stopped at the top of the expansive marble stairs. On either side of them giant white pillars stood at regular intervals.

"And this book will show conclusively that a very powerful force from the past was at work," came Lovell Madeira's voice from their left. "And I shall be personally available at Fanelli and Company Booksellers for an exclusive signing on January fourth . . ."

The microphone was switched from Lovell to Jewel Coleman, who began asking him questions. A cameraman hovered in front of them.

"He's having a blast, isn't he?" Kelly said, giggling.

"He's not the only one," Jupiter said. He indicated a circle of people off to the right. In their midst was another camera, focusing on Manny Firestone.

"And what better topic for a thriller than this very story itself?" he bellowed into a mike. "I lived it—I should know! So that's why I commissioned the very best playwright of our time to do a show about it. We call it *Inside the Danger Zone*, and it's a winner! We're starting ticket sales in a month, but you can place phone orders now!"

Pete groaned. "Here we go again!"

"Huh?" Kelly said.

"This isn't the first time someone's promised to dramatize one of our cases," Jupe explained. "Although last time it was going to be a thriller-diller movie."

Just then there was a scream from a group of teenagers at the bottom of the stairs. They began stampeding up toward Jupiter and his friends.

"Autograph hounds," Jupiter said, rolling his eyes. "I'm just not in the *mood*."

He forced a smile and prepared for the worst. But they went straight for Pete, smiling and holding out autograph books.

"Guess they heard you, Jupe," Kelly teased.

"Well—I—just because they went to Pete *first*→"

"Hey!" a wide-eyed girl shouted to Jupiter. "Weren't you in the show?"

Jupiter gave Kelly a triumphant smirk, then turned to the girl. "Why, yes, I was. But I seemed to have neglected to bring a pen—"

Before he could finish, the girl turned to a friend and said, "Remember him?" She rounded her arms and extended them to the sides, then puffed out her cheeks and crossed her eyes. Waddling awkwardly on the steps, she chanted, "The beachball! The beachball!"

One by one her friends joined in.

Jupiter suddenly wished he were in Hawaii.

Pete gave him a sympathetic smile and shrugged his shoulders. "Well, Jupe, you always did want to ditch the Baby Fatso image."

Watching his imitators bounce down the stairs, Jupiter gave his friend a withering look. "Thanks a lot, Pete. You really know how to make a guy feel good."